About the author

Scott McKenzie lives and works in Manchester, UK. In addition to writing fiction, he also writes for dvdactive.com

Praise for Rebirth

Scott McKenzie's *Rebirth* is a real page-turner that leaves you hungry for more from this new writer. If you aren't absolutely thrilled by the exciting chase sequences and the bloody confrontations, the charm and wit of the characters will win you over. Spinetinglers highly recommends this book for anyone who loves classic vampire tales with a modern twist.

www.spinetinglers.co.uk

AF472332

Scott McKenzie

Rebirth

First published in 2007

Copyright © Scott McKenzie 2007

ISBN 978-1-84753-412-5

This novel is a work of fiction. Names and characters are the product of the author's imagination and any resemblance to actual persons, living or dead, is entirely coincidental.

Rebirth was published on the internet in 2007 at
http://rebirthnovel.blogspot.com

Contact the author:
s.a.mckenzie@gmail.com

Cover title typeface
Dirty Ego by Misprinted Type
http://www.misprintedtype.com

For Lizzie

Acknowledgements

I wish to thank everyone who has proof read *Rebirth*. Your participation has been invaluable and has given me the confidence to publish this novel.

I also wish to thank those who have subscribed to the blog and you, for picking up this book and taking a look inside…

Prologue

1
One Year Ago

He was frantic.

The straps binding his arms and legs gave way and he leapt to his feet. The figures standing round him were frozen in shock. Before they could attempt to hold him down, he bolted for the door and ran faster than he had ever run before. Something was flowing around his body, carrying him at a speed he never thought possible, something that had been explained to him many times before that he didn't want to believe.

He was in pain. Incredible agony.

There was a fire in his stomach. The pain stabbed him in the belly and he doubled over, stumbling into the wall. Using his hands to steady himself, he got back onto his feet and continued his dash for freedom.

The shouts of his captors echoed behind him.

'Don't let him leave! He can't be allowed to escape!'

'Shoot him if you have to!'

'No! Take him alive.'

'It's too late, doctor. He's beyond help now. There's nothing more you can do for him.'

He was dead.

He was sure of that already, but if he could make it down the long stone-flagged corridors to the front steps and make a leap for it, he might have a chance of survival. Two figures appeared in front of him but he immediately barged them out of the way, sending them skidding along the smooth floor. Just in front of him were the heavy doors that stood between him and the outside world.

He paid no mind to the possibility that the doors might be locked. Without a pause to think about his actions, he felt all the power in his body flow through his arm and up his side and shoulder-charged the wooden barricade, knocking it from its hinges. The cool fresh air washed over his face as the rain poured in torrents from the darkness above onto the gravel drive and lush green lawn ahead of him.

As soon as his feet left the top steps, he heard a gunshot behind him. He kept running down the steps onto the drive and wondered why there were no more shots. Then he lost all feeling in his chest. He put his hands to his heart and knew what was happening. As he fell to the ground with his life ebbing away, the voices of the men who had held him against his will for so long and done hideous things to him rang in his ears.

'There goes another one.'

'We've learned a lot from him. I think we know what we have to do.'

'How long will it take to reach the next stage?'

'Give me twelve months.'

Part One

Setting Sun

2
A Stranger Approaches

Present day

The fifth day of the heat wave was coming to an end and the sun was overstaying its welcome, casting long shadows of the city skyline across the freeway towards the suburbs. The commuters lucky enough to own air-conditioned vehicles sat in relative comfort while others peeled the sweat-drenched shirts from their backs as they inched their way home.

The late September sun finally dropped out of the sky just before nine o'clock, taking with it the blinding light but leaving behind the stifling, sticky heat. Every store that stocked electrical fans had sold out of them much earlier in the week and local air conditioning businesses were doing their best end-of-season trade in years.

One man who didn't have the heat wave on his mind was driving a lone black car along the freeway into the city. He had specific orders: the first was get to his destination as quickly as possible but stick to the speed limits. Do not attract any attention. The whole cause would be in jeopardy if the authorities were alerted to his mission or, worse than that, if *they* found out what was going on.

A gloved hand changed gear and the other steered the car towards a large industrial complex. The driver stopped the car next to the security booth and hit the button to roll down the blacked-out window. The security guard got off his chair for the first time since the sun went down and shook himself free of his damp uniform. It immediately stuck to him again, feeling uncomfortably cold and wet.

'Putting in some overtime, Doc?' the security guard asked, hoping for some friendly banter to bring some respite to the tedium of the long night ahead. 'Can you believe this heat? Should be at home with a cold one but here I am, working for the man.'

He hoped for a clever reply but didn't even get a boring one.

Oh well, some people are just like that, especially people like Doctor Owen here who works all the hours God sends, he thought to himself.

In the low light, he couldn't see the driver's face but he'd lost count of the number of times he'd waved that badge through after hours so he didn't think there was any point in making a fuss.

'You're clear to go, Doc. Have a good night.'

The driver nodded and continued his drive up to the front door of the research labs of Mantek Pharmaceuticals. He picked a black briefcase off the back seat and stepped out of the car.

The bright white light that illuminated the reception of the Mantek building spilled out into the darkness of the car park. The man carrying the briefcase walked up the steps and through the front door with a purpose. His long dark shadow slithered into the building behind him.

Time to carry out the second order.

3
Mission Accomplished

Danny Johnson was a young research assistant, working away quietly in one of the many labs at Mantek. All the other labs were empty, which pleased Danny. He found it a lot easier to get work done with no one else around. All day long, other scientists and assistants were popping in and out, borrowing samples and equipment or asking for advice. This way, there were no interruptions.

His supervisor, Andrew Owen, had been eager to leave early that afternoon so Danny was more than happy to do some overtime. Doctor Owen's boss, Doctor Forrest, hadn't shown his face in the lab for a while. Danny had heard them talking about a breakthrough and it surprised him that he hadn't seen more of them that week and that he was left in the lab to do all the hard work.

What the hell, may as well stay in the ice cool lab than brave the heat outside and get some extra cash at the same time.

Anyway, the quicker he did the work, the more overtime he could claim and profit from. A little white lie never hurt. He had only been left with simple instructions of what to do. Doctor Owen had not told Danny the relevance of what he was doing; only that he had to put some of the yellow liquid in the blood samples, look at it through the microscope and save the images to the lab computer.

Easy money.

For the last time that night, Danny put a drop of blood onto a thin glass slide and clipped it under the microscope. He looked into the microscope and saw the same thing he had seen all night: human blood with a high level of white blood cells but lacking in red blood cells and haemoglobin. He hit a button and heard an artificial camera click as the computer grabbed the magnified image and saved it to the hard drive.

Very carefully, he picked up the pipette from the flask of yellow liquid, dropped it onto the blood sample and looked back into the microscope. He had no explanation for the reaction he was watching but it had become more familiar to him as the night wore on.

Let the doc try and work out what's going on, I've had enough for one night.

Danny hit the button again to capture the image of the reaction and rubbed his eyes as he looked up from the microscope. It was reaching ten o'clock and Danny decided to call it a night.

He was starting to pack the equipment away and put the blood samples back into the refrigerator when he saw a silhouette block the light from the small window in the laboratory door.

'Hey, Jeff, is that you?' shouted Danny.

Jeff was the security guard that did the rounds twice a night. He had a good relationship with all of the insomniac scientists. Like many pharmaceutical companies, Mantek had problems with animal rights protestors and they had to keep a watchful eye out for infiltrators. Just six months earlier, a whole lab full of rhesus monkeys had been set free by an animal liberation group, most of which ended up under the wheels of trucks on the main road outside. The irony was not lost on the employees of Mantek but it didn't stop the protestors trying again when the new batch of primates arrived just days later.

Danny didn't receive an answer to his call.

The door handle slowly turned and the door opened just a fraction. White light from the corridor illuminated a hand that reached inside and flicked the light switch. Just before the lights went out, Danny saw something left behind on the light switch from the stranger's finger: a drop of blood.

'Hey, what's going on? Who are you?' he asked, raising his voice this time.

Still no answer.

The door opened wide. A tall, dark figure took a step inside the lab, set a black briefcase down on the floor and closed the door behind him. Before Danny could adjust his eyes to register what was happening, he was plunged back into darkness.

'What do you want?' Danny's voice broke a little.

The dark stranger shot across the room and grabbed Danny's head in his massive gloved hands. Danny punched the man's sides with all his might but he didn't flinch.

'Where is the doctor?' the stranger demanded in a deep, rasping voice.

'Doctor Owen? He went home.'

'Don't lie to me. He's not at home. Where is he now?'

'I don't know. Probably in the city somewhere but he didn't tell me where he was going. I really don't know where he is.'

That was the last thing Danny said before the stranger squeezed his hand and bent the young lab assistant's head into an unnatural position, quickly breaking his neck with a sickening crack. The stranger released his grip and Danny's limp body slumped to the floor between the refrigerator and the filing cabinet.

The stranger picked up the black briefcase and carefully placed it on the workbench in the middle of the lab. He clicked the briefcase open and flicked a switch inside then quickly made his way out of the door and down the corridor. In exactly five minutes' time, all traces of his visit and the doctor's work would disappear in a ball of fire.

That wasn't the end though. Doctor Owen was still out there somewhere in the city. For the sake of the cause, everything depended on him being found before *they* got to him.

The stranger walked through the reception area of Mantek, past the dead body of Jeff the security guard lying face down on his desk and out to the car. As he threw the Mantek surveillance tapes onto the back seat, his mind was on the third and final order. It was as simple as the first: get back without attracting attention. Once he had taken care of the security guard waiting in the booth at the front gate, there would be no evidence that he had visited Mantek.

Mission accomplished.

But this is only the beginning.

4
One Star Motel

The clock on the dashboard clicked round to midnight as the rented saloon pulled into the car park of the Lone Star motel. There were plenty of parking spaces to choose from. The saloon came to a stop and the tall, thin figure of Doctor Andrew Owen stepped out.

A concrete box with thirty or forty rooms in it, Doctor Owen thought as he surveyed his surroundings. *Architecture straight out of the low point of the seventies.*

Above the entrance, a grimy sign pointed the way to a swimming pool at the rear of the motel. Doctor Owen would bet his bottom dollar that all the pool contained was two inches of green slime but suspected there wasn't anyone here that would take his bet.

Lone Star Motel? One star motel would be a more appropriate title, he thought, half expecting the capital L to fall off the sign. *Still, beggars can't be choosers and when you've got to lie low, there's nowhere lower than the sewer.*

Doctor Owen checked in and paid for his room, which was unreassuringly inexpensive. Without getting out of his seat, the desk clerk handed him the key and went back to watching the tiny colour TV sitting on the desk.

What an easy job, Doctor Owen thought, *I'd give anything to swap places with you right now. You can have all my money, all my qualifications and all the secrets I know.*

All I want to do now is put my feet up, watch TV and forget about everything.

But he couldn't do that and he knew it. He had a responsibility to his wife, his friends and everyone he worked with. Hell, he even had a responsibility to the kid sitting there watching TV without a care in the world. That responsibility was to stay alive and finish his work.

For the first time in his life he was glad he didn't have any kids. The doctor and his wife Emily had considered it for many years but as was the case with many other aspects of their personal life, his work came first.

Emily had left him several times but always returned. She knew that living with the potential saviour of the human race would be difficult. It wasn't as if he was a sex-addicted lothario or a clandestine alcoholic. When they were together, he was a model husband: caring and considerate, and they both thought they would have been perfect parents.

They had argued and cried about having children countless times but they always came to the same conclusion: once his work reached this stage, they would be in mortal danger and it would have been selfish for them to think the safety of the children wouldn't be affected by his work. She remained loyal to him and he prayed that she had remained safe since they temporarily parted earlier that day.

Warm, musty air and the stale, lingering stench of cigarettes hit Doctor Owen in the face as he opened the door to room thirty-seven. As expected, what stood before him was a basic motel room: a bed, a TV and a bathroom. Everything he needed for the night. Tomorrow he would check into another motel and attempt to make contact with Doctor Forrest, who led the research assignment.

He threw his bags on the patch of the mustard carpet that held the fewest stains and went into the bathroom. He splashed cold water on his face and looked at himself through the film of dirt on the mirror.

Am I really the saviour of humanity? Can I live with the responsibility?

He decided it was too late and he was too tired to be contemplating the meaning of his life so he threw himself on the barely clean bed sheets and fell asleep almost immediately.

Deep in sleep, Doctor Owen didn't hear the door handle click and a floorboard squeak as a heavy size eleven stepped inside. Nor did he hear or see a tall dark figure approach the bed. The only thing he noticed was a tight grip on his neck a split second before a chloroform-soaked rag covered his face.

5
Jane

The green glow from the digits of the alarm clock lit the corner of the room. Sitting on the bedside table were a purse, a mobile phone, a compact of makeup that was rarely used, a silver DKNY watch and a swipe card giving the highest level of access to the World Health Organisation's global offices.

The name on the card was Jane Simpson.

Strictly tools of business. No wedding ring. No engagement ring. Not even a number in the mobile phone that wasn't work related.

Jane was lying in the comfort of her king size bed, sound asleep in her pink satin pyjamas. Her head was buried in a pile of pillows and cushions, the covers thrown to the floor hours before to let her body cool down. She was halfway through a two-week vacation and hadn't felt this relaxed for years. The project she was involved in wouldn't come to fruition for another few weeks so she had allowed herself the time off.

Once the current phase of the project was complete, there would be a lot of work to do. Very dangerous work.

Even in her unconscious state, she knew that she had another whole week of reading, watching black and white movies and that old favourite that she never had time for: retail therapy. Maybe one day in the not too distant future she would even have time to call the guys that gave her their numbers. She'd have to find those business cards first though. They were probably somewhere under a pile of papers somewhere…

Then, just when all seemed rosy in the life of Agent Jane Simpson, her mobile phone started to ring. Her eyes opened and she sighed when the reality check kicked in.

Why the hell didn't I turn it off?

She rubbed her eyes and looked at the alarm clock. Two in the morning. *Wonderful.* She answered the phone and heard a familiar voice on the other end. It was the voice she had expected to hear but really hoped she wouldn't: the manager of the emergency response team. She had lost count of the number of times they had spoken to each other at this ungodly hour.

'They've got him,' he said. With that, she sat up in her bed. She was now one hundred percent awake.

'What about his work?' she asked.

'Destroyed. His office at Mantek has been bombed. We need you to find out what happened. A lab assistant was murdered so we'll need to get the police department in on this as well.'

Jane got to her feet and opened the first door of her massive wardrobe to reveal her collection of work clothes. She had enjoyed not having to open this door every morning for the past week. Now it was time to get back to work.

She wasn't looking forward to working with a cop. They never shared the same priorities. The World Health Organisation was completely focused on tracking the spread of known diseases and aiding the search for a cure. Cops only wanted to solve the crime, in this case a murder, or at least find some poor sucker to pin it on.

It was important that she got on the scene as quickly as possible. That way she could get all the necessary investigation underway before one of the local boys in blue turned up and slowed her down by sticking his nose in.

'I'm on my way. I'll be there in twenty minutes.'

6
Stakeout

Jesus Christ, it's hot.

I'd been sitting in my car since long before the sun came up, waiting for our suspect to emerge from his house. A mixture of caffeine and the drone of commercial radio were helping me to stay awake. I didn't know for sure if he was even here but his car was in the drive and none of our grasses had seen him out and about for days.

On the hour every hour, the newsreader on the radio reported on an attack at a pharmaceutical company. A lab had been bombed and three people had been killed. They didn't say too much about it though. That was typical of this city. It's an unfortunate reality that there would probably be more deaths on these streets before sunset and the bombing would be old news by the end of the day.

I thought I saw something or someone move inside the house so I lifted the binoculars off my lap and peered through them. The house was in a state of disrepair. Every visible piece of metal was coated with rust and the front gate was hanging off its hinges. Across the picket fences that needed a new coat of paint and the lawn that was slowly getting out of control, I checked each filthy window. Nothing moved. I lowered the binoculars and closed my eyes for a second.

I must be losing my mind. Get a grip, Tom.

If I hadn't missed out on a promotion last year, I would have been sitting there with the air conditioning blasting away. Superficial I know, but it's one of the perks of being a senior detective. Come to think of it, if I hadn't missed out on a promotion last year, I would have been sitting in a comfortable office with the air conditioning blasting away. Apparently I was too valuable doing what I was doing so my boss couldn't let me go.

In my experience, bosses don't give a shit about you but as soon as you want to do something different and they realise you're actually useful to them, they come up with some half-assed compliments about you being a critical member of the team and make up some bullshit about new challenges which keeps you doing the same job for another year.

That's right; no one can sit outside suspected murderers' houses all day long waiting for them to come out then kick them in the balls and read them their rights better than I can. Not that I don't enjoy that part of the job to a certain extent but that's not the point. I felt like I needed something new in my life.

I cracked open my second can of a disgustingly powerful energy drink and gulped it down in one. A shudder went down my spine and I shook my head involuntarily. *These drinks can keep you awake when your body tells you it's time to go to bed but why do they have to taste so bad?*

The passenger door opened and my overweight partner, Detective David Thomas, shook the car as he crash-landed in the faux leather passenger seat. Luckily the two cups of coffee in his hands had lids on the top otherwise we would have ended up wearing the contents.

'Here you go, Tom,' he said in his slightly high-pitched voice. 'Get that down you, you'll feel better.'

'Thanks, Dave. I'll probably be pissing all day with all this liquid but I feel a bit better now. What, no doughnuts?'

Dave laughed. 'The last thing you need is more sugar, partner. Anyway, my diet starts today,' he added with a wink.

He was right. It was just after eight in the morning and this was my third coffee of the day. A double espresso. I hadn't slept for a few days. Well, not during the nights anyway. Dave reckoned it was because of all the coffee I drink. I knew he was right but by the time I feel like sleeping, I'm back at work.

I'd been up for days, reviewing endless security tapes. I eventually found footage that showed who had beaten Andre Lewis, a nightclub bouncer, to death. The killer is usually one of the first people we talk to and this case was no exception. The details weren't important to me any more though. I had three very simple steps to follow:

Step 1 – Arrest this guy.

Step 2 – Take some time off.

Step 3 – Sort out the life of Detective Tom Ryder.

Dave lurched forward in his seat and snatched the binoculars out of my hands. 'The curtains just moved.'

I looked across the street and saw the curtains of the small suburban house move. It was the first movement we'd seen since the sun went down last night. We had slept in shifts. Well, Dave had slept; I just closed my eyes and tried to fight the thoughts that were buzzing around in my head, keeping me awake.

'Could be the wind,' I suggested.

'The windows are closed.'

I picked up my gun, checked it was loaded and clicked the safety off. Dave did the same. Time for him to ask me if I'm ready.

'Ready?'

'Always,' I replied, as usual.

The front door of the house swung open. There stood our suspect in his pyjamas and slippers; a very short, stocky man, only five foot two but almost as wide. We had to be careful. He had managed to beat a man to death with his bare hands who was a clear foot taller than him.

I was psyched. My heart was pounding and I felt adrenaline surging through my veins. Even though it didn't seem possible, I started to sweat even more. I had to take this man down, for the sake of society and more importantly, for my own sanity. This man stood between me and a good night's sleep.

I picked up the radio and announced, 'This is Detective Ryder. We have positive confirmation of the location of the suspect. We're moving in.'

'Let's go,' Dave said.

We bounded out of the car and shot across the street, pointing our guns at the suspect.

'Police! Don't move!' I shouted.

The suspect looked shocked and tried to make a run for it but his freedom didn't last long. I shoulder-charged him into the wall. He stayed on his feet for a second but a swift boot to the balls sent him tumbling into his flowerbeds. My trusted size tens haven't let me down yet.

Dave leaned over the squirming suspect with one knee firmly digging into his back. 'Give me your hands,' he said. 'Do you watch Cops on TV?'

'What? Er… yeah, sometimes.'

'Good, you already know your rights then, asshole. Keep still.'

As Dave handcuffed the suspect, I returned to the car and picked up the radio. 'This is Detective Tom Ryder. We have apprehended the suspect in the Lewis killing.'

'Well done Detective Ryder,' was the reply, 'we'll prepare a nice uncomfortable cell for him back at the station.'

'Thanks, we're on our way.'

I breathed a sigh of relief and watched Dave drag the suspect towards the car. I felt the weight of the world start to lift off my shoulders. My vacation and my sanity were within touching distance.

7
Tom

The suspect was very well behaved on the ride to the station, sitting quietly and staring out of the window, weighing up his fate. We had to lock all the doors and roll up the windows just in case he decided to make a run for it so the car was hotter than ever as the morning sun burned through the windscreen.

I didn't care though. I was tired, hungry and emotionally drained. In a few hours I'd be able to go to bed and I wasn't planning on moving from it for at least a week.

'Do you mind booking him in on your own?' Dave asked.

'Why? Have you got something better to do?'

'Yeah, I've booked some vacation and it's due to start this afternoon if I've got nothing else on.'

'Yeah, no problem,' I said, 'What are you doing with your time off?'

'Taking Janine and the kids away', he said, 'We're going up to the lake. I'm going to teach the boys to fish.'

'Are they old enough to go fishing?' I asked.

'Pete, the eldest, he just turned nine last week,' he corrected.

'Time flies,' I said, hoping to cover up my faux pas, 'seems like yesterday you were rushing off to the maternity ward.'

'It certainly does. Twice as fast when you've got kids. I'll be packing them off to college before I know it.'

Dave was a good family man, married for God knows how many years with three kids. He was one of the only people I counted as a true friend and even though we had worked together on and off for many years, he had only been my official partner for the past six months.

He talks about his kids all the time but I get mixed up with the names and we've known each other far too long for me to ask him to remind me which one's which. If I had a girlfriend or wife, I'd ask Dave and his wife round to my place for dinner. As it happens, I'm single and planning on staying that way so I don't suppose they'd be too interested in coming round to my apartment for Heineken and TV dinners.

I was married once, a long time ago. Her same was Sarah. We were very happy together, right up to the day she told me she hated me and wanted me to move out. She told me I was spending too much time on my work and not enough with her. We had endless arguments about it but she was right.

She gave me the choice of my work or her but didn't let me make the decision. As soon as I paused to think about it, she knew what the true answer was and walked out of the door without saying another word.

The marriage lasted five years, which isn't too bad in this day and age, or so I keep telling myself. Looking back, I guess I wasn't really husband material and when I look in the mirror, I realise I'm even less suitable now than I was back then. I always wanted kids but wasn't sure why. Probably because that's what everyone's brought up to believe in. Go to school, get a job, get married, have kids, retire, have grandkids, die. That's the way it's supposed to go, isn't it? Looking back, it's probably a very good thing for the kids that I didn't get past the 'get married' stage.

One day Sarah called and told me she wanted us to get back together. I was ecstatic. I moved back into our apartment and took as much time as I could off work so we could spend quality time together like normal couples. When I went back I took a desk job, started at nine and walked out of the door dead on five every day so I could get home to spend as much time as possible with my beautiful wife.

Everything was going well until Michael Hudson was released from prison.

Michael Hudson was the first murder suspect I arrested early in my career in homicide. He caught his wife cheating on him and took revenge on her with a baseball bat. After beating her body for over an hour, almost all of her bones were broken and her entire body was bruised and bloody. He then went to the kitchen, made himself a cup of coffee and went to visit her lover to do the same to him.

He received a twenty-year sentence but served only nine years. They said he was released for good behaviour but as far as I knew, he hadn't done anything in prison that I would consider good behaviour and certainly hadn't given enough back to the community or the justice system to warrant giving him eleven years of his life back.

On the day of release from prison, most people visit friends, a bar or a brothel. Michael Hudson went to a sporting goods shop, bought a baseball bat and paid a visit to our apartment. I wasn't at home but

Sarah was. She didn't stand a chance against nine years of pent up aggression.

He was given a life sentence with no chance of parole for twenty years. I still don't know if I would have preferred the death sentence. I'm the one who caught him and I always thought there would be closure once he was out of the picture.

I was wrong.

Every day for the last five years I have thought of different ways to take it all out on him but nothing could bring back what he took away. Even though he's probably going to be locked up for the rest of his natural life, every day I expect to get the call to say he's got a release date.

After he was put away, I threw myself into my work. I don't always play by the rules and I'm not in the job to make friends but I always get results. My investigations have led to more convictions for homicide than any other detective in the department for the last three years. I've tried talking to the department shrink but that didn't do much good. It only made me think about what happened to Sarah so I just blank it out the best I can. That's why I turned myself into a workaholic: so I don't have to think about the life Sarah and I could have shared.

Being a detective is pretty much the same as doing any other job I guess. It's hard, boring work with the occasional moment when you realise why you decided to take the job in the first place. Today's arrest was one of those moments.

Our hard work had paid off and now after two long, exhausting weeks of dead end leads and waiting around for forensic evidence, I was standing at the front desk of my police station booking in the prime suspect in a murder case. He was set to go before the judge the next day and I suspected he would either be refused bail or it would be set way out of his price range.

Someone else would have to interview him. Dave had already disappeared and I wouldn't be around for another two weeks. Dave deserved the time off and so did I.

8
'Sorry Tom…'

It was all going too well. I knew I should have avoided talking to my boss.

'Sorry Tom', Captain Nash started, 'I've got some bad news for you.'

I was standing in the Captain's office, listening to him try to tell me my vacation had been cancelled in the longest, most roundabout way possible. Another crock about me being the best detective he's got and how he can't do without me.

I knew what he was trying to say the second he opened his mouth: that my vacation was being cancelled and I'm sure he knew that too but for some reason he felt the need to talk around the subject for several minutes first.

If bullshit were pennies, this guy would be a millionaire.

'If I'm that great then give me a raise, Captain,' I said once he'd finished telling his story. A completely futile suggestion but I wanted to make him squirm even more.

'Look here Detective, just about everyone who's got a family has booked time off and the ones that didn't have called in sick.' He was shouting at me as if it was my fault, like I was in the wrong because I had the nerve to want to take some time off work. Men with families always got the holidays they wanted and I had to pick up the scraps that were left over. That pissed me off.

I should have known though, it was a predictable situation. Good weather always causes people to call in sick. They pretend they've been laid up for a few days but when they get back to work they've got golden brown suntans. It's at times like this when I think the world is full of lazy bums and hard working men like me and my partner Dave are the exception rather than the rule.

'That's not my problem, Captain,' I protested, 'if half your men phone in sick on a sunny day you need to get them in here or fire them. Read them the riot act, for Christ's sake!'

'You know I can't do that so I'm afraid it is your problem, Tom. I've got dead bodies stacking up all over the city and no one to find out who put them there. God damn it, I wish the situation was different but it's not.'

My mind was filling with anger and desperation. One emotion was about to bubble over but I didn't know which one.

'I need some time off, Captain,' I pleaded desperately, 'I've been working all day and night on the Lewis murder. Now I've cracked it, I've got to get some sleep. Period. You can't ask any more from me.'

'Sorry Tom, you'll need to try and get some sleep tonight. Right now I need you to get over to Mantek at the other end of the city.'

He could have at least tried to look like he was sorry but his expression didn't change at all. In his mind we got to take vacation as a bonus rather than a right. There was no point arguing any more, I didn't have any choice. If I protested any more, I'd be heading for suspension or worse. Taking this case was the last thing in the world I wanted to do.

'I heard about the attack on Mantek on the radio. What happened?' I asked, resigned to my fate.

'Someone walked in last night, killed two security guards and blew up one of the labs. A young lab technician was working there at the time.'

'Dave's on vacation. I take it I'm alone on this one?'

'This one's different. It falls under the jurisdiction of the World Health Organisation. Apparently the lab was being used to research the cure for some disease. The WHO have got the whole place quarantined. Your contact will be Agent Jane Simpson. She's already on-site.'

Great. I get to work with a woman. No doubt someone else who'll end up hating me.

The case itself didn't sound too bad. Most likely animal rights activists and there were only two of those groups with any significant presence in the city. *Shouldn't take too long to ask around and find out who the angriest members of the groups are.*

'Any suspects?' I asked.

'You now know everything I know, Detective.' I made a point of asking him for more information every time I got a case, even though he never knew anything of any importance. I thought that one day he might realise all he did was bark orders without giving me anything to work with but that day hadn't come yet. I doubted it ever would but I hoped he would prove me wrong.

'I don't have any choice, do I Captain?' I asked, with desperation in my voice.

'You know the answer to that one, Tom,' he said, staring deep into my eyes. 'You know the score. You're the best man for the job. I'd rather have you running at fifty percent than half the other guys running at a hundred percent.'

That would be flattering if it wasn't a total fabrication.

'I'll do this for today but you'd better get someone else lined up because I'm calling in sick tomorrow,' I announced.

'Sure you are,' he replied, knowing that I was bluffing.

I turned round and left his office, slamming the door behind me. That was it. Forget about your vacation, Tom. Get out there and get back to work.

It's hard work being the best.

9
Reflection

Screw them all, I'm going home, I thought as I passed my apartment on the way to the crime scene. My foot hit the brake pedal and I turned the car around. I had to at least freshen up before taking on a new mission.

What the hell, I'm going to be working with the World Health Organisation for the first time. Better make a good first impression.

I would have tried to convince myself that Captain Nash might agree with that logic if I cared one way or the other.

I stopped the car on yellow lines at the side of the road and hopped out. It's one of the few perks of the job: no one ever gives a cop a parking ticket. Well, no cop ever pays the fine anyway.

There was no air conditioning in my block so there was no relief from the heat as I walked through the front door. The lift was broken as usual so I took the stairs up to the fourth floor and had to take a second to catch my breath when I got to the top.

I really need to sort myself out if I'm going to stand any chance of doing myself justice today. I could do with visiting the gym as well. They've been taking my money on the first day of every month for the last two years so I should really start getting my money's worth some time soon.

There was a familiar aroma as I opened the door to my apartment. I call it home. Every home has a distinctive smell. It just so happens that I'm the only person who appreciates my apartment's distinctive smell.

I peeled off my suit and shirt and dropped them in a soggy pile on the floor. In the corner of my eye, I caught the sight of my bare body in the long mirror on the wardrobe. I hadn't taken a good look at myself for a long time.

I had to do a double take, I was so shocked.

Do I really look like that? *Where did that gut come from?*

I prodded my stomach and it wobbled. Only a little bit but I definitely saw a wobble. Last time I looked, that chest was tight. I used to play squash three times a week for Christ's sake! I'm sure the six-pack was still under there somewhere but a soft cushioned layer had appeared from nowhere.

Looks like I'm built for comfort rather than speed these days. I looked down and saw the dusty handle of my old squash racket poking out from behind the wardrobe. There was no doubt in my mind: I needed to sort my life out.

I walked into the bathroom and as my feet stuck to the floor, I registered the fact that I also had to sort my apartment out as well. I couldn't remember the last time I gave the place a thorough cleaning. To be honest, I couldn't remember the last time I even gave the place a light dusting.

I stepped into the shower and closed my eyes, letting the hot water rain down on me. I hoped it would wash away the pains like it had washed away countless hangovers over the past five years. I was sober now though. I hadn't had a drink for over a week.

Eight days and counting.

I turned off the shower and took a second to gather my thoughts. Rubbing the water out of my eyes, I knew the pain was still in my mind. The urge to sleep for a week hadn't subsided but the rest of my body felt a bit better than it had since last Tuesday, probably because I hadn't had a shower since last Tuesday.

I got out of the shower, dried myself off and looked at myself in the mirror again.

At least I look refreshed even if I don't feel like it.

In the mirror, I caught sight of a bottle of Jack Daniel's sitting on the coffee table. It had one shot left in it. It was the only bottle left in my apartment that contained any alcohol. Gordon's, Captain Morgan, Bacardi, Smirnoff, Jose Cuervo. They were all empty. Gone and well and truly forgotten.

All that remained was the bottle of Jack and a shiny shot glass. The day I pick up that bottle and that glass would be the day I took a step back down the path I swore I would never walk again. I hated myself when I was drunk but only slightly more than when I was sober. At least the time went quicker when I was drunk.

It was the time when I wasn't working that I hated the most. When I was working, my mind was active and I could take my frustrations out on my surroundings, whether it was an over-zealous arrest or some argumentative banter with Dave and the Captain.

The pain really started when I was unfortunate enough to finish work early and return home with nothing to do, especially when I wasn't tired enough to immediately pass out when I crashed onto the sofa. That was the point when my sleep needed a helping hand from my good friends Gordon, Jose and Captain Morgan.

I wasn't the type of drunk to go out on the town, blow all my money and pick a fight. I preferred to sit on the sofa with a bottle in my hand and look at old photos, watch old home movies or just think about the happy times I shared with Sarah and wish we'd had more. Just a sofa, a bottle, my memories and me. Once I started drinking, I could find no reason in the world to stop until Mother Nature sent me off to sleep.

The reason for Sarah and I not spending more time together was always me. Every time we were going out for dinner or round to friends' houses, I would get *the call.* There was yet another killer on the loose and it was always up to me to find them and lock them up. Noble work to be sure, but not conducive to marital bliss.

The friends we used to have had abandoned me long ago. Needless to say they were all Sarah's friends rather than mine. Of course, they all rallied round after she died and stuck by me for a while but I guess I should be the first to admit that my attitude probably pushed them away rather than drawing them close when I needed them most.

I kept staring at the bottle of Jack. One sip and that was it. No more work. I could start drinking now and kiss goodbye to the next two days.

The devil on my shoulder thought it sounded very tempting.

Pull yourself together, Tom!

I marched over to the drinks cabinet, picked up the bottle and unscrewed the top. I picked up the shot glass and looked at it for a second before throwing it into the metal dustbin by the door. There was a satisfying smash when it hit the bottom. I went back into the bathroom and emptied the last shot of Jack into the sink then smashed the bottle in the dustbin.

Goodbye old life, hello new beginning.

10
A Meeting Of Minds

I arrived at the front gates of Mantek headquarters to find the whole place in chaos. There were reporters and TV vans all over the road outside the complex. No one from the media was allowed onto the grounds but that didn't stop the photographers climbing the walls to get front-page pictures for the late editions.

As the security guard waved me through the gate, cameras flashed like strobe lights all around me and reporters banged their microphones on the windows asking for a comment. It felt like I was driving through a riot. The car belonged to the department though so I didn't care about the bumping and scratching as much as I probably should have.

Even from the entrance at the opposite end of the grounds from the research building, the extent of the damage was obvious. It was quite a sight. A large chunk of the Mantek research building was missing, like someone had taken a huge bite out of the corner where the lab used to be. It immediately occurred to me that it would have taken a large quantity of explosives to do that much damage.

I drove up the tree-lined road towards the research building and saw crowds of people in white biohazard suits going in and out. As I reached the end of the drive, a security guard walked up to my window.

'What's your business?' he asked.

'Police. I'm here to meet Agent Jane Simpson,' I said.

'You're the detective, right? She was waiting around for you but you're late so she might be in the building.'

'Late?' I asked. *Who does this jobsworth think he is, telling me when I should have arrived? I only took on the case an hour ago.*

'Yeah, she was expecting you half an hour ago.' The look on his face made me think I was back in school, being put in detention for turning up late for registration. It was Captain Nash's fault. What an asshole. He must have told them I was coming before he even talked to me about the case.

'Carry on straight ahead and park next to that big white van', he continued, 'she won't be far away.'

I parked the car and started asking around for Agent Simpson. It wasn't long before I was pointed in the direction of a woman talking to a group of men in white biohazard suits. For some reason I was expecting a middle-aged woman in horn-rimmed glasses but I was a little shocked when I saw her. She had dark brown hair tied in a short ponytail and was about five foot six. Her biohazard suit restricted any further assessments I could make apart from the fact that she was young and pretty. Well, younger than me anyway.

I must have looked out of place because she walked over as soon as she spotted me. 'Agent Jane Simpson. Pleased to meet you,' she said and extended a hand to me. 'You must be the detective.'

'That's right. Detective Tom Ryder,' I replied as we shook hands. 'Looks like you've got a lot of work on your hands.'

'A lot of work on *our* hands, Detective,' she said. 'I've got a suit for you in the van. You're coming in with me.'

I guess that's the end of the pleasantries. Time to get down to business.

'What happened here?' I asked, 'I didn't get much information at the station.'

'It looks like someone didn't agree with the research that was going on here. The lab was being used to work on the cure for a highly contagious disease of the blood. That's why we need to be suited up.'

'What about the hole in the side of the building? Shouldn't that be covered up to stop the contagion spreading?' I suggested, trying to ask her something relevant.

'No, that's not a problem. The disease isn't airborne; you can only catch it by coming into direct contact with it.'

'What's the disease?'

'Nothing you'd have heard of. It's very rare and Mantek want to keep it that way.'

Nothing I'd have heard of? She's not scared to speak her mind. I'd probably be offended if I didn't think she had already worked me out.

'But you know what the disease is, don't you?' I asked.

'Yes,' she said, 'I've dealt with it before.'

'Who were the victims?' I asked.

'Two security guards and one lab assistant. We'll need the police department's help to perform the post-mortems.'

'That's fine; just send the bodies down to the hospital,' I said, 'Any ideas who might be responsible? Anyone got a grudge against the company or the people who work here?'

'Mantek has the same problems as any pharmaceutical company,' she said, 'There are the usual attacks on employees and their families by animal rights activists but this doesn't fit the profile. You need to see the lab for yourself. Better get suited up.'

She grabbed a white suit out of the back of the van and threw it to me. It was made from inch-thick rubber and I let out an involuntary grunt as I caught it. The midday heat was becoming uncomfortable already but the suit magnified the temperature as soon as I stepped into it.

'Jeez, it's going to be hot in here,' I said, pointing out the obvious.

'There's more bad news,' said Agent Simpson, 'the explosion knocked out the air conditioning system and the engineer can't get in to fix it until we're done.'

And the hits just keep on coming.

11
On The Spot

Agent Simpson led the way into the entrance hall. We walked through a huge gap in the walls left behind by her colleagues after they had removed the glass doors to facilitate their movements in and out of the building. Inside, the forensic team were carrying out a body bag. I asked Agent Simpson what had happened.

'That's the security guard's body,' she said, 'He took a beating then his neck was broken. The perp did nothing to hide the body.'

'It must have been a swift operation if he left the body lying there,' I said. Agent Simpson nodded in agreement.

On the way up to the lab on the second floor, we passed several men in suits taking samples from the floor, the walls, anywhere that might hold some evidence of who did this or the type of explosive they used.

The rubber suit squeaked with every movement and the heat inside was already unbearable. I was beginning to question the wisdom of stopping home for a shower and change.

We entered the lab through an irregularly shaped hole in the wall where the door used to be. It was a complete mess from floor to ceiling. I couldn't believe that someone had been happily working there just twelve hours earlier. A massive hole had been blown in the outside and inside walls and we could stand on the edge of the room and look outside at the people working below. Papers and fragments of scientific equipment were strewn all over what was left of the room. Ash and dust covered everything. It was going to be difficult to get any decent forensic evidence out of this room but in my experience, if you take enough samples and do enough tests, you nearly always get a lead.

I cast my eyes around the room, taking in as much as I could. It was very important to me not to judge the crime scene on the first thing I looked at. An easy trap to fall into is to pick one thing at the crime scene and focus solely on that, when there might be several other clues screaming out at you in another corner.

'What are your first thoughts?' Agent Simpson asked after only a few seconds, putting me on the spot. No doubt someone had told her I was 'the best' so she probably wanted to test this theory herself. Now it was my turn to sound like I knew what I was talking about.

'The destruction wasn't caused by something small like a hand grenade,' I said, 'Whoever did this wanted to make sure there wasn't any forensic evidence for us to sift through. We can use the explosive residue to find out what they used but that's going to take a long time.

'In my opinion, this explosion was intended to cover up what went on in here, not to send a message. I agree with you: it's unlikely that animal rights protestors did this.'

Two forensics officers were carrying a body bag out of the room. 'What happened to the kid?' I asked.

'His body was found behind the equipment over there,' she said, pointing to a fire-damaged refrigerator and filing cabinet, both twisted out of their natural shape, 'Not all of his body was destroyed.'

'Which means that he was lying back there, either dead or unconscious when the bomb went off.'

She nodded in agreement. 'His body is on the way to the morgue.'

'Good, we'll need to get down there and take a look at it. I saw security cameras around. Has anyone taken a look at the tapes?'

'The tapes are usually stored at the front desk but they've gone missing. It's likely they were taken when the perp left the building.'

'Who else works in this office?' I asked.

'Doctor Forrest and Doctor Owen are the scientists who run this research lab. We haven't heard anything from either of them.'

'See if you can find their home addresses,' I said, 'I'll send a patrol car round to pick them up.'

'Do you think they were the intended targets?'

That seemed like an odd question to me. Not because what she was asking didn't make sense, but because I would have expected anyone to jump to the conclusion that the scientists who ran the lab were in danger. It seemed like common sense to me.

'Whoever did this targeted this lab for a reason. They wanted to stop the research and even went so far as to kill the lab assistant and the security guards, probably only because they were in the wrong place at the wrong time.

'Their work may have been stopped but these scientists still have the intellectual capital. They could start their work again in another lab.

If the bomber was prepared to go this far, we have to assume the scientists are the next targets.'

12
The Brotherhood

About ten miles outside the city limits, in several hundred acres of woodland, stands the majestic Hartley House. The magnificent stately home was built by a local farmer called Alexander Hartley when farming was the best way to make a million, long before Lotto and reality TV shows created new millionaires every week.

The farmer became incredibly rich through years and years of toil and ended his working life a satisfied and accomplished man. Unfortunately, on his day of retirement he realised that because he had worked so hard all his life, he had nothing to spend his money on. No wife, no children, no hobbies, nothing at all.

All he had was his house, so it became his life. He made the house his reason to get out of bed every morning. He kept building and expanding the mansion, adding more and more rooms until eventually it became one of the largest private residences in the world.

Many successful business people had owned and lived in Hartley House down the years until one of the owners became unexpectedly unsuccessful and had to hand it over to the government to pay off his tax bill. It then became a hotspot for schmoozing important persons of influence who were visiting the city.

On this day, it wasn't being used for schmoozing. In fact, you wouldn't have set foot in Hartley House in over a year unless you were a member of The Brotherhood.

In one of the many splendid-looking halls, two men in camouflage gear and masks were fighting each other with long silver swords.

One man was noticeably taller and wider than the other and obviously more skilful with the sword. His name was Captain Stein. His opponent was Private Brown. To be fair to Private Brown, he was holding his own. Captain Stein had beaten him into submission numerous times in the twelve months they had been posted at Hartley

House. He had also beaten him numerous times when they were posted at the other end of the country for six months.

Before joining The Brotherhood, Private Brown had been working in a fast food restaurant after dropping out of school. He was a damn good burger flipper back then and was determined to be just as good with a samurai sword as he was with a spatula. He met Captain Stein on the night his parents were killed and signed up to The Brotherhood in a shot.

The sparring practice followed the same pattern as it usually did between Stein and Brown: Stein was permanently on the attack and Brown spent the whole practice session frantically defending. The only difference was that it took Stein longer than usual to knock the sword out of Brown's hands. But knock the sword out of his hands he did, and then followed up with a kick to the knees that sent Brown tumbling to the floor.

They both removed their masks and Stein helped Brown to his feet. 'Good effort, Brown,' said Stein in a strong, booming voice. 'Now tell me what you did wrong.'

'Same as usual, Sir,' Brown replied. 'All I did was defend. I didn't get the chance to attack.'

'Wrong, Brown. You didn't make the chance to attack,' said Stein as he tapped Brown on the head. 'Your problem's in there. You have the ability but you're not channelling it. We'll try again tomorrow.'

'Thank you, sir,' said Brown.

They saluted each other and Brown left the room. He passed Commander North in the doorway. Commander North was another big, burly man like Captain Stein, only with more experience written in the lines on his face.

'I know I don't need to ask the result,' North said as the men saluted each other. 'You have a good man there, Stein. Is there any news?'

'Yes sir. The lab was bombed last night. The doctors' work was completely destroyed.'

'What happened to them?'

'They've both disappeared but we've got a team going out to find them today.'

'I want you to lead the team. You can find them. I have every confidence in you.'

'Thank you, sir. We will leave immediately.'

They saluted each other. On the way out of the room, Commander North left Stein with a parting shot. 'Remember, if you don't find the doctors, we're all dead.'

13
Dead Easy

There are many things not to like about being a homicide detective: finding the body of someone you know, telling a mother her child has been killed and knowing who the murderer is but not having enough evidence to put them away, but top of the list is the autopsies.

I don't consider myself a squeamish person. I can deal with most of the dead bodies at crime scenes but it's the scientific detail of autopsies I find difficult to stomach. Twenty-four hours earlier, the two people in front of me were living and breathing and shared their lives with people who loved them. Now they were just clues that hopefully contained some evidence and we were going to pull them apart to find it.

I stood over the body of Jeff Jones, the Mantek security guard with Agent Simpson and Doctor Joseph Schreiber. Doctor Schreiber was our forensics expert. He was a good guy, one of the few people I work with that I might consider a friend, but we had met on too many occasions.

'Dead easy this one,' said Doctor Schreiber. I had heard that line on too many occasions as well. Agent Simpson hadn't heard that one before though and I was sure I saw a smile in the corner of her mouth. 'He was beaten around the face for a while before the neck was broken.'

I looked the body up and down and noticed something odd. 'There aren't any marks on his hands. No bruising on the knuckles.'

'You're right,' said the doctor.

'What does that tell us?' asked Agent Simpson.

'He didn't land a punch,' I said, 'he took a beating and died without fighting back. Sitting behind the desk, he must have seen his attacker coming but was overpowered very quickly.'

'The attacker was undoubtedly very powerful and a skilled combatant,' said the Doctor Schreiber, 'look over here though, the other body is even more interesting.'

We turned around to look at the partially charred remains of lab assistant Daniel Johnson. Apart from the unnatural angle his head was positioned, the top half of his body was relatively unscathed. His legs were a different story. The flesh had melted away and all that remained on the bones were charred muscles and tendons.

'As you can see, there's not much evidence we can get from the lower half of the body but the burns aren't as bad across the torso. The spine is broken at the neck and there is also additional dark bruising around the neck area, as you can see.'

Doctor Schreiber pointed out long and thin bruises on one side of the neck. 'A large hand probably made these marks.'

'Do you think he was choked?' Agent Simpson asked.

'It looks like it,' I replied, 'he must have been choked then had his neck broken before the explosion.'

'That's right,' said Doctor Schreiber, 'there are no indications here that the explosion killed him. While the burns he sustained to his legs and body are severe, he would have had a fair chance of surviving. If he had been directly in front of the blast, the whole lab would have been decorated with his body.'

I saw Agent Simpson's nose turn up at that thought.

'So his death was not accidental,' I continued, 'and the attacker was probably in the building just before the explosion.'

'I agree', said Doctor Schreiber, 'these burns were sustained to a body that had only just expired.'

I looked at Agent Simpson and saw her nodding in agreement with what we were saying. She seemed hard working and intense which can usually add up to bloody-mindedness but she appeared to be receptive to our conclusions. Maybe working with her wouldn't be too bad.

Her phone rang and she answered it. She took a pen and pad out of her jacket and wrote something down then hung up. 'That was from the team at Mantek,' she said, 'We've got the address for Doctor Owen.'

Things were really moving along. At this rate, we'd have the investigation tied up by dinner time. *I might be able to take my vacation after all.*

'Let's go,' I said as I headed for the door, happy just to be on my way out of the morgue.

14
Another Cuppa

'I haven't heard a thing from him since last night. Do you think he was hurt? Do you think he went back to the lab after he left me?'

Emily Owen was in a state of panic. Andrew's Auntie Becky was doing her best to keep her in a positive state of mind but a lack of sleep and an overdose of caffeine were not helping matters at all. She wasn't really Andrew's Auntie and Emily couldn't remember how they were related but they both thought she was sufficiently far-removed to allow her to lay low for a few days until Andrew found a safe place for them to stay.

'Watching the news isn't going to help,' said Auntie Becky as she turned off the television. 'They haven't said anything about Andrew so he couldn't have been caught up in it, not like that poor boy he worked with. No news is good news, Emily.'

'You're right. But it doesn't stop me thinking the worst.'

'I know, dear. Do you want to go into the other room and try and get your head down for a few minutes?'

'There's no point. I feel tired but I wouldn't be able to sleep.'

Auntie Becky looked at the empty coffee mug on the table in front of Emily.

'Another cuppa then?' she smiled.

Emily handed the mug to her. 'If you've got any coffee left. We've been through a lot today.'

'You let me worry about that, dear.'

Auntie Becky left the room and Emily reflected on what a great help she'd been. She was always warm and welcoming to them but she had really gone over and above family duties in the past twenty-four hours.

Andrew had called Auntie Becky to ask for her to look after his wife and she hadn't asked one question about the situation, even when they heard of the attack on Andrew's lab. All she knew was that Andrew was in trouble and the people he worked with might come and want to take Emily away. Even the police weren't to be trusted, but Auntie Becky thought that was taking the story a bit too far. Her late husband had been a police officer after all.

Emily couldn't say anything about her real fears. If the news had reported that Andrew's body had been found at Mantek then at least she would know what had happened. It would be tragic of course, heart-breakingly tragic, but she knew his fate could be worse. Much worse.

Many years ago Andrew had confided in her a secret that he had sworn on his life never to tell another soul. He gave her the choice to leave on many occasions but she couldn't do it. She decided to give up what she wanted out of life to support the man who could change the world for the better. There wasn't a day that went by when she didn't question the wisdom of her decision but she told herself that it was for the best.

Look at the bigger picture, Andrew always said.

Her thoughts were interrupted by the screech of tyres outside. She immediately got up and ran through to the kitchen.

'Becky, are you expecting anyone?'

'No, dear. Why?'

'There's someone at the door.'

'Are you sure?'

At that moment, the doorbell rang.

15
Front Door

The tyres of the two black vans screeched as they came to a halt outside a house in the pleasant leafy suburbs. The sliding door rumbled as it flew open and allowed fresh air to enter the leading van. The men inside felt some relief from the stuffiness of their uniforms.

Captain Stein stepped out and checked out his surroundings. Just as he had suspected, it was a *nice* area of the city. He suspected his ex-wife lived somewhere like this with that bastard surgeon husband of hers.

Keep your mind on the job in hand, he told himself.

No one had heard anything from Doctor Owen since the destruction of the lab. Stein knew the chances of finding the doctor or his wife sitting comfortably at home were practically nil but with two missing scientists to find, they had to start at the beginning.

Stein had always had his suspicions about the doctor. Their paths had crossed several times and there was always an atmosphere between them, like they both questioned each other's motivations. He had voiced his concerns to his superiors many times and just recently they had started to listen.

Find the doctor, then we'll make sure his work gets back on track, they had said.

One of his men in the van offered his rifle but Stein refused. 'Leave it there. I've got my pistol in my belt. It's the middle of the day. We can't run round waving our guns about unless we have to. The same goes for all of you. Leave your rifles inside.'

The soldiers all nodded and put their rifles under their seats.

'Wait here for now. Don't make a move unless I give you the signal or you see me draw my pistol. Got that?'

They all nodded again.

Stein walked up the drive to the front door, glancing through the windows on the way. He couldn't make out any movement inside, but it was difficult because the glare of sunlight on the glass obscured his view into the house.

Faced with the front door, he popped the clip that secured his pistol in his belt with one hand and rang the doorbell with the other.

16
'Come With Me'

'I can't let anyone take me away. Andrew told me…'

'I know what he said, dear,' said Auntie Becky, 'don't worry, I'll go and see who it is and get rid of them. I bet it's just someone trying to pressure an old lady like me into changing my gas supplier. Go and wait in the bedroom.'

Without making a sound, Emily sneaked up the stairs and into the bedroom where she would have liked to have slept last night and sat on the edge of the bed. She left the door open slightly so she could hear what was going on downstairs.

It's not as if I can do anything up here if they've come for me, she thought. *Andrew said they knew a lot about us but he was so sure the people he worked with would take a long time to work their way through the family tree before they got to Auntie Becky.*

Becky watched Emily disappear up the stairs then went to answer the door. *I'm sure this is a lot of fuss about nothing*, she thought, *Andrew has always been the eccentric of the family.* That was the reason she didn't put the security chain on the door before she opened it and it was also the reason she invited the man at the door inside.

'Hello officer,' she said, 'what can I do for you? Do come in, it's boiling out there.'

The policeman at the door stepped inside. 'Thank you ma'am, it certainly is.'

What is she doing? Emily thought, *Andrew told her not to trust the police.*

'Can I get you anything, officer? Something cold to drink? My husband was a police officer and he always hated the summer. Much preferred the winter. At least then you can get into the car and warm up. He always said it was easier to warm up than cool down.'

'Your husband sounds like a clever man. No thank you, ma'am, I can't stay for long. I'm looking for a relative of yours, Emily Owen. Have you seen her in the last twenty four hours?'

Don't do it, Becky. Don't tell him I'm up here.

'I have seen her, officer. As a matter of fact, she's just upstairs.'

Damn you, Becky.

'Do you think I could have a word with her, ma'am?'

'Of course, officer. Emily! Come down. Don't worry, it's the police.'

Knowing there was nothing she could do to get out of it, Emily got to her feet and edged her way down the stairs but stopped halfway.

'Hi, Emily. Is Doctor Andrew Owen your husband?'

'That's right.'

'Okay. I take it you know about the attack on your husband's lab last night.'

Emily nodded.

'And have you seen him since?'

Emily shook her head.

'We've got some questions for you. Can you come down to the station?'

'Why can't you talk to me here?'

'I don't want to impose on your relative here. It's best for everyone if you come down to the station with me.'

'What if I don't want to go with you?'

'Like I said, Mrs Owen, it's best for everyone if you come with me.'

17
Shadows

Two more black vans belonging to The Brotherhood bounced over the speed bumps on the long drive up to a large house shaded by tall trees. On the outskirts of the city as the suburbs turns into countryside, another squad of soldiers had only one objective in their collective mind.

Find Doctor Forrest.

No one had seen or heard from Mantek's head of research for a long time. Any time The Brotherhood had tried to dig deep into the life of Doctor Forrest, it appeared that he didn't have one. No family. No friends. Just his work and nothing else, which was always encouraging when he was working for them, but when he goes missing it is very difficult to track someone down that no one knows.

Lieutenant Curtis sat in the passenger seat of the leading van, gripping his rifle tightly. He had his sights set on a captaincy and if this mission was a success, he had a good shot at getting a promotion. His radio fizzed and he heard the familiar voice of Captain Stein.

'Curtis, are you there?'

'Yes sir.'

'Have you reached your destination?'

'We're just pulling up now, sir. Have you made contact?'

'Negative. There's no one at home. We turned the place upside down but found no leads. It's only a matter of time before the police start looking for the doctor so we have to keep moving down the list. Let me know as soon as you have control of the situation.'

'Yes sir.'

The vans stopped in front of the stone house and the soldiers jumped out onto the gravel drive. Lieutenant Curtis led the men up to the front door and noticed it was ajar. The feeling that something might be wrong started to grow in his stomach.

Did they *get here first?*

He pushed the door open and took a step inside, feeling the cool air bite his skin. The trees surrounding the house captured the sunlight and he heard a low hum in the background that he suspected was an air conditioning machine. The interior and furniture were black and dark brown. Blackout blinds covered all of the windows. Coupled with the temperature, the atmosphere was a stark contrast to the day the rest of the city was having.

Lieutenant Cutis waved his hand and the soldiers split up and slowly moved silently into the many rooms. As the last soldier made his way into the house, a shadow shot out of a dark corner and the front door slammed behind him, plunging the squad into near darkness.

A few shots were fired, but as quickly as they had entered the house, the squad looking for Doctor Forrest were dead.

18

One Step Behind

There was time to reflect on the day's events as I drove us along the haze-covered streets towards Doctor Owen's house. We had gathered the following facts so far: last night someone walked into the Mantek building carrying a bomb. He or she, most likely a he, killed the security guard at the front desk with very little resistance then went into the lab, broke the lab assistant's neck and set off the bomb, which was much more powerful than a regular Joe could easily lay their hands on.

The question was why? That would surely lead us to the killer. The answer had to lie in the work being carried out in the lab, which only Doctor Owen or Doctor Forrest would be able to shed some light on. Doctor Forrest was also still missing so my hopes for a quick resolution lay with this chance of finding Doctor Owen.

Agent Simpson had been repeatedly trying to call Doctor Owen on the phone numbers that her colleagues had provided us with, but there was no answer at his house and his mobile number went straight to voice mail.

Why can't we contact him? Is it because he doesn't want to be contacted or was it because he can't get to a phone? Is he in danger? Surely he isn't responsible for last night's attack, is he?

I've known some detectives to go crazy during complex investigations. There are so many questions, so many possible scenarios that it can feel like the pieces of the puzzle will never fit together. If you couple that with the pressure put on you by senior officers and a detective's own sense of urgency, a case can get very stressful very quickly. I've learned to keep my questions and suspicions in the back of my mind and only draw conclusions when I have plenty of facts and evidence.

Jumping to conclusions in this business is very dangerous, especially where people's lives are concerned. It's not an approach that is always appreciated by my superiors: they want results and I've known other detectives to plant evidence just to get a conviction to meet their targets, but I want to get my man the right way every time.

Since Sarah's death, I've had a one hundred percent record. It's the one thing in my life that makes me proud of myself.

'His car's in the drive,' Agent Simpson remarked as we pulled up outside Doctor Owen's three-floor townhouse. This was one of the less dangerous parts of the city. Homicide investigations don't lead me to this area very often. Most of the time I'm sneaking around dark corners in the projects looking for gang-bangers. This upper class area was a lot easier on the eye but the job in hand was not very different.

We got out of the car and I led the way. In the corner of my eye I could see curtains twitching in the next-door neighbours' house as we walked up the drive. I had forgotten the different effect that a police presence has depending on the area. In the projects, everyone in the neighbourhood runs into their homes, locks the door and keeps their heads down but in a nice area like this, the residents can't wait to see their neighbours get taken away by the cops.

I knocked on the door a couple of times but there was no answer. I couldn't hear a sound coming from inside so we headed round the back of the house. I peered through a window to see that bookcases had been thrown to the floor and cushions were ripped open. I couldn't see any signs to tell me that anyone was still in the house.

Something was happening in this city and it was happening very quickly. I got the feeling we were going to stay one step behind all day unless we got a major breakthrough.

Agent Simpson looked over my shoulder. 'Oh my God, what's going on, Detective?'

'Looks like someone beat us to it,' I said as I drew my gun.

I kicked in the door at the side of the house on the first attempt and we made our way inside, into the kitchen. The place was a complete mess. All the cabinet doors had been ripped from their hinges and it looked like anything not nailed down had been smashed on the floor.

'Anyone there?' I shouted and waited a few seconds.

Nothing.

'We'd better not move any further,' I said, 'it's likely the bomber has been here so we need to get forensics down here. Do you have a picture of Doctor Owen?'

'Yes, I got one from Mantek. Why?'

'We need to put the word out to all units. We've got a missing person to find. I just hope that whoever is doing this hasn't got to him first.'

19
Short Cut

Within half an hour, the forensic team arrived at Doctor Owen's house so we left them tagging and bagging everything that looked like it might hold some evidence that would lead us to who was doing this. There was so much stuff to go through and so many rooms in the doctor's house, they would be there for hours.

We were in the car, heading back to the police station to talk to Doctor Owen's wife Emily. She had been staying with a relative and it was only a matter of time before she was found and taken into police custody for the sake of her safety. So far she hadn't said a word on the subject of her husband's whereabouts but I was hoping to break her down.

I looked in the mirror and noticed a black saloon hovering about fifty metres behind us. I hit the brakes and turned the car down a street to the left. I'd been followed enough times to be able to spot a vehicle on my tail.

'What are you doing, Detective?' Agent Simpson asked, clearly rattled by my impulsive driving.

'It's a short cut,' I lied.

We turned off the main road and the black saloon followed us. I swung the car to the left again and as expected, the saloon followed.

'But we're going back on ourselves,' Agent Simpson protested.

'Trust me,' I said, and heard her sigh, like she knew I wasn't going to tell her what was going on. She looked in the wing mirror and started to turn round to look through the back windscreen.

'Don't turn around,' I said, 'there's a car on our tail.'

Agent Simpson looked in the wing mirror again. 'The black one?'

'That's right.' I picked up the radio and kept an eye on the registration plate of the following car as I spoke.

'This is Detective Tom Ryder. I need a name and address check on the following registration plate: Whisky Seven Four Seven Bravo X-ray Charlie.'

'Okay Detective, I'm on it,' was the reply on the radio.

'Detective!' Agent Simpson shouted.

'What?' I asked. I took my eyes off the rear view mirror and looked at the road ahead, immediately realising what Agent Simpson wanted me to notice. I'd been looking in the mirror at the car behind for so long, I hadn't noticed the traffic was slowing down in front of us. I slammed on the brakes and we both lurched forward, the seatbelts just holding us in our seats. The car screeched to a halt just behind the car in front. 'Sorry about that,' I said.

I looked in the mirror and the car tailing us had disappeared. *Damn.* I just hoped the address check came back with a useful lead. After a few moments of uncomfortable silence in the car, a reply came on the radio: 'The car is registered to a Doctor Forrest at one-two-four Castle Crescent.'

'That's at the other end of the city,' I said, 'is there a black and white that can stop by that address? A missing person may be at that address. Proceed with caution and do not approach the target until we get there, target is a possible abduction victim.'

'Understood. I will get back to you when a patrol car is on site.'

I turned the car around in the middle of the road, narrowly missing some of the traffic, rolled down the window and stuck the portable siren on the roof. I found the ramp onto the ring road and jammed the accelerator to the floor, dodging in and out of the vehicles and onto the freeway.

'Do you really think he's been abducted?' Agent Simpson asked.

'I think we have two options,' I said, 'Either Doctor Owen blew up his own lab and did a runner or someone else did it and abducted him. Which one do you think is more likely?'

'I see. Is that what's called a cop's hunch?'

'Not really. This is about playing the odds. We need to proceed as if Doctor Owen and Doctor Forrest are both in danger and we have to assume we can get to them first.'

'Why?'

'Because if we don't we'll probably have four homicides to investigate rather than the two we've had so far today.' A thought occurred to me. 'Do you want me to drop you off? You work for the World Health Organisation, not the police. This is probably going to get dangerous from now on.'

'No, don't worry about me, Detective,' she replied very quickly, 'I've been in worse situations.'

'The World Health Organisation must be more exciting than I thought,' I said. To be honest, I had no opinion on the WHO at all. For all I knew, they sat around in offices all day long, reading reports and deciding which rat-infested restaurants to close down next.

'You've no idea,' she said cryptically with a sly smile in the corner of her mouth.

'The patrol unit has arrived at the address,' said the voice from the radio, 'please advise.'

'Do not approach the house, we're nearly there,' I said as our car bounced down the off-ramp. 'Only observe for now and do not take any action unless there is a life in danger.'

20
Doctor Owen

The blackout curtains hadn't been completely closed, allowing a little sunlight to spill into the room. The furnishings were expensive: an orthopaedic emperor size bed, a huge walk-in wardrobe and very deep carpets.

As Doctor Owen awoke from his chloroform-induced slumber, he cast his eyes around the room and instantly knew where he was. One-two-four Castle Crescent.

Why am I in the boss's old house? He hasn't lived here for years. How did I get here?

He was gagged and tied to a chair in Doctor Forrest's bedroom. It occurred to him that he was alone. The last thing he remembered was booking into a motel a hundred miles north of the city and getting his head down. He knew this was coming but had hoped to make a better run for it and finish off his work before *they* found him.

He wasn't supposed to tell anyone the full details of his work but his wife Emily knew everything.

Please God let her be safe. I'll never forgive myself if anything happens to her.

The next question was *where is Doctor Forrest?*

Is he gagged and bound to a chair in another house somewhere else? Is he in this house? Is he dead? What about his family?

All these questions and more buzzed around his head, but his thoughts were interrupted when a tall figure suddenly burst into the room. The figure ran over to the window and closed the curtains.

There was very little light illuminating the room and all Doctor Owen could see was a huge frantic shadow. The shadow turned to the doctor and growled, 'Don't move or make a noise or you're dead. Understand?'

Doctor Owen didn't move a muscle, knowing exactly the fate that would be in store if he didn't comply. This was the first time he had knowingly come face to face with one of *them.* The atmosphere and attitudes did not surprise him one bit.

'Good,' said the shadow and left the room, slamming the door behind him.

Something's happening, Doctor Owen thought, *is someone coming to rescue me?*

21
'Check Your Weapons'

Captain Stein felt like he was being baked alive as he sat in the back of the cramped black van. It was one of two vehicles carrying a squad of soldiers who were speeding along the freeway. Their destination: the home of Doctor Forrest.

How many homes does this guy have? He hasn't lived there for years, or so we thought. What else don't we know about him?

Stein thought of the squad that had gone to the address they had for Doctor Forrest and feared the worst. He suspected he would never hear from Lieutenant Curtis again.

Little did the police know that The Brotherhood had been listening in to their conversations all day long. This Detective Ryder seemed to know what he was doing and he was leading them directly to Doctor Owen, one of the principal members of their scientific research team. Stein almost felt sorry for the detective. So much hard work, it was always a shame to steal a cop's thunder.

The Brotherhood had used this tactic many times before but this time may be more difficult than usual. If their vans didn't reach the house first then they would have the police to deal with in addition to the likely presence of *them.*

Captain Stein shouted to the driver. 'How long to go?'

'Only two or three minutes,' said the driver.

'Okay,' Captain Stein announced to everyone in the van, 'check your weapons and put your masks on.'

The soldiers all loaded their rifles and pulled black balaclavas onto their heads, wiping the sweat from their foreheads before they did so.

It had been a long time since Captain Stein or any other members of The Brotherhood had seen this much action. The Brotherhood had co-existed with *them* in a stable state for the past twelve months.

He had known all along that everything would change once Doctor Owen made progress in his research. They all did. The doctor was the key to the future of every living creature on the planet.

Captain Stein checked his rifle one more time as the van headed down the ramp, leading them off the freeway and into the tree-lined roads of the suburbs.

22
New Partner

Five minutes later, we pulled up next to the patrol car hiding around the corner from one-two-four Castle Crescent. Sitting in the car was Officer Greg Myers. He was a good cop and we'd worked with each other before on several occasions. He'd picked the best spot on the road: most of the vehicles driving past wouldn't see him at a glance. If there was anyone in Doctor Forrest's house, there was a fairly good chance they didn't know we were here already.

Officer Myers and I got out of our cars and shook hands.

'Good to see you, Detective,' he said.

'You too, Officer. How have you been?'

'Pretty good. Should be going for detective soon.'

'Really? Which division?'

'I think I might go for homicide.'

'Good choice,' I said. What's more, I meant it too. Officer Myers would make a very good homicide detective. He's smart, good with people and never scared to kick down a door with no idea what's on the other side. When you've got to tell people their friends and relatives are dead, you've got to be good with people. I'd found that part of the job pretty difficult since Sarah was murdered.

'I suppose you'll need a new partner soon,' he continued.

'No, I'm still on the same partner I had last time we spoke.'

My partners have a tendency for getting shot. Or worse. It's not a secret either. Some potential partners have volunteered for demotion or redundancy rather than work with me. That kind of sentiment from potential partners doesn't exactly give you a warm fuzzy feeling inside but after a few years you just get used to it.

'Wow, he's lasted at least six months! Well, why don't you use this opportunity to try me out? It might help to get me further up the waiting list when your current partner has had enough.'

'Okay,' I said reluctantly, 'lead the way but I have to warn you, it's a very short waiting list.'

'Can I do anything?' asked Agent Simpson.

'Yes, wait there and keep the engine running,' I said, expecting another sigh.

'Okay detective,' she said and saluted me.

Hang on a minute, is she flirting with me? I'd almost forgotten what that was like.

We walked across the road towards the house. There were no people around and no cars cruising up and down but I was sure I saw some curtains twitching in neighbouring houses for the second time today. The trees lining the long crescent swayed in the light breeze, which was a relief in the current heat wave.

I stood at the bottom of the steps at the front door, staying alert while Officer Myers pressed the doorbell. There was no answer so he tried the door handle. It opened and we drew our guns. Very slowly, he led us inside.

We were faced with a very plush upper-middle-class house. The carpet was so soft and expensive-looking I almost thought I should have taken my shoes off before going any further. There were gold fittings on the furniture and even though I had no idea who painted the pictures on the wall, I suspected they were originals or at the very least limited edition prints. A stark contrast to the cheap sofa, Dali prints and wafer-thin rug in my apartment.

I pointed upwards and Officer Myers edged his way up the stairs. I looked up the stairs and noticed that it was unnaturally dark up there. This struck me as very weird considering the blazing sunshine outside.

Rather him than me, I thought selfishly as I made my way into the kitchen at the rear of the house.

23
Keeping The Engine Running

Agent Jane Simpson sat in the car with a hundred thoughts buzzing around in her head. *Keep the engine running*, Detective Ryder had said, assuming something bad might happen meaning they would have to make a quick getaway.

If only he knew what they might have to make a quick getaway from.

Only Agent Simpson knew what might happen and she hoped to God it wouldn't. He seemed like a nice guy under that difficult exterior, but most importantly he was a good detective and was her best chance of finding Doctor Owen and Doctor Forrest before *they* did.

Come on, she thought, *just get in the house, pick up the doctor and get out.* It would be a lot easier for everyone. Detective Ryder and Officer Myers stepped inside the house and she knew they didn't have long.

They would be coming. *They* must have heard the conversations on the police radio. *They* wouldn't be as subtle as these two though.

She looked out of the window and saw a pair of black vans driving down the crescent. Her heart sank. She sat rigid as she watched the vans stop outside the house. The doors immediately swung open and three men wearing black suits and masks jumped out of each one. They were all carrying machine guns.

One of the men stopped and looked around. He stared directly at Agent Simpson and gave her a wave. She raised a hand and he ran towards the house to join the others.

What can I do? If she sounded the horn to warn the men inside, these soldiers would almost certainly kill her. *Her colleagues.* If she got out of the car to try and stop the attack, her cover would be blown and they'd be back to square one if the doctor wasn't in the house. She didn't have Tom's mobile phone number, but should she call him even if she had it?

She just hoped that Detective Ryder could find a suitable hiding place somewhere in the house and stay there for the duration of the attack.

If he doesn't, he's a dead man.

24
Screams

The sequence of events seemed like a blur at the time but now I know things went like this.

Officer Myers went up the stairs and I crept into the kitchen, pointing my gun at anything and everything.

'I've found him!'

I heard the shout from upstairs followed by the sound of a door opening. This was quickly followed by another shout from Officer Myers, only this time it was a blood-curdling scream of agony.

Then there was a smash of glass and I spun round to see a canister fly through the small window in the front door. It hit the ground in front of me and thick white smoke started to pour into the room.

What the hell is going on?

Without thinking, I turned around again and ran into the kitchen, looking for some cover. I ducked behind the kitchen worktop and kept my head down.

I heard the front door burst open and at least two mask-muffled voices that I suspected were well trained in military operations.

'The noise came from upstairs.'

'You two head upstairs, we'll cover the ground floor.'

Two sets of footsteps charged up the stairs and two more started to get louder as they moved towards me.

'We have him. We also have a man down, looks like a cop.'

'Holy shit!'

There was a deafening blast of machine gun fire followed by an unholy scream.

'Confirmed kill. All other rooms are clear. Looks like there's only one of them here.'

'Better not take any risks on the victim. Finish him off.'

I heard another short blast of machine gun fire.

'Pick him up and let's get out of here.'

The footsteps bundled down the stairs again.

'Good work, men. Let's go.'

I waited for a second then slowly peered over the top of the worktop. I couldn't see if they had left or not because smoke had filled the entrance hall and was starting to creep into the kitchen. I knew I had to take a chance.

I got to my feet and ran over to the sink, picked up a cloth and ran it under the tap. Covering my mouth with the damp cloth, I made a run for the stairs, hoping I wouldn't bump into one or more of the armed intruders or succumb to the effects of the smoke. Luckily for me, there was no one on the other side of the thick white cloud.

When I got to the top of the stairs, I saw massive smouldering burns on the walls and a pile of ash on the carpet. Officer Myers' body was lying in a pool of blood. His neck was wounded, with dark red blood pouring from his neck and soaking into the carpet. His back was peppered with bullet holes.

Covering my mouth from the fumes that were creeping upstairs, I made my way back down to the hallway and out of the front door to see two black vans screeching away from the house. Agent Simpson got out of the car and I met her in the middle of the road.

'What happened? Who were they?' she asked.

'I've no idea but whoever they are, I think they've got the doctor.'

'I think you're right. I saw them bundle someone into the van. What happened to the cop?'

'Dead. They shot him but something else was going on before they arrived. I don't know what happened in there. Call for backup. I'm going after them.'

25
Call From Stein

As Detective Ryder disappeared around the corner to the sound of squealing tyres, Agent Simpson stood on the lawn of Doctor Forrest's house and watched the tear gas pour out of the front door and disappear.

She took her mobile phone out of her pocket but before she could call for police backup, it began to ring and she recognised the number immediately. Captain Stein.

'Stein,' she answered, 'have you got the doctor?'

'Yes we have, Agent Simpson. It was a surprise to see you just then. Sorry about your boyfriend.'

'He's on your tail right now.'

'What do you mean? We had to kill the cop.'

'No, there were two of them. Detective Ryder was in the house as well. You must have missed him.'

'Shit. And he's right behind us?'

'Yes, he drove after you as soon as you left.'

'I think I can see him. Thanks for your help, Agent Simpson.'

'How is the doctor?'

'He seems okay. A bit shaken up after being locked up with *them* but we'll have him back at Hartley House very soon. He keeps babbling about his wife so we'll send someone round to pick her up.'

'Too late. The police have already picked her up.'

'Damn it. It's going to be hard to get hold of her now. See if you can get her out of the police station.'

'I'll do what I can.'

'Good. Right, I'm going to have to take care of him now. I'll try not to kill your new boyfriend.'

'Go easy on him, Stein. He's got us this far.'

With that, the line went dead.

26
Catching Up

The vans had a head start but I was confident of catching up with them. I had no idea how I was going to apprehend half a dozen armed and well-trained soldiers, if that's indeed what they were. I jumped in the car and hit the accelerator, turning the corners I think they may have taken.

I picked up the radio. 'This is Detective Ryder calling Dispatch.'

'This is Dispatch. Go ahead.'

'I need to find two black Chrysler vans that left Castle Crescent two minutes ago heading East, carrying an abducted man who holds information vital to the bombing of the Mantek building last night. Get the chopper on the case.'

'I'm afraid that's not possible, Detective. The helicopter is currently tracking a runaway vehicle on the Expressway.'

'Jesus Christ, do you mean we've only got one chopper?'

'That's affirmative, Detective.'

'Well make sure all local units keep their eyes peeled.'

'Understood, Detective.' The radio clicked off and back on again. 'All units in the vicinity of Castle Crescent and the Parkway stay alert. We are looking for two black Chrysler vans heading east. Repeat…'

'Don't bother repeating,' came another voice from the radio, 'this is unit one-five-two. Two black Chrysler vans have just gone past me on the Parkway. I'm now following them. Please advise.'

'Do not pull them over,' I said into the radio, 'they are heavily armed. Continue to follow and I'll find you. Dispatch, come in.'

'This is Dispatch. Go ahead.'

'I need you to send a tactical aid unit to intercept the vans on the Parkway.'

'Understood. ETA five minutes.'

I made it onto the Parkway, one of the many long roads leading from the city centre to the suburbs. I stuck the siren on the roof and ran all the lights, narrowly missing a few of the less observant commuters. Then I saw the vans in the distance, about half a mile down the road, closely followed by a patrol car.

'Unit one-five-two, I'm right behind you.' I said.

'What's the move, Detective?'

'Keep on their tail. A tactical aid unit should be here any minute.'

I dropped a gear and floored the accelerator. Dodging in and out of the commuters, I quickly caught up with the patrol car and pulled in behind the vans.

'Detective Ryder is it?' came another voice from the radio.

'This is Detective Ryder.'

'Stop following us. Call off the tactical aid unit.'

Damn it. They've been listening to us the whole time, probably all day. That's why they turned up at the Doctor's house just after we did.

'Who are you? What do you want with the doctor?'

'That is none of your business.'

'You killed a friend of mine back there so I'm making it my business.'

'Trust me, Detective, he's better off dead.'

'Do you have Doctor Owen in your custody?'

'Yes we do,' he replied, 'but he's much safer with us than he could ever be with you. Back off now and no one else will get hurt.'

I kept on the tail of the vans and moved my car closer.

The back doors of the rear van opened to reveal a man in a black military suit with a radio in his left hand and a machine gun in his right, looking directly at me. Two more men in black suits were sitting behind him but I couldn't see Doctor Owen in there.

'Maybe I didn't make myself clear,' he said into his radio, 'back off or I'll make you back off.'

'You won't shoot me. It's broad daylight and you're heading into the city at rush hour. Where will you go?'

'Again, that's none of your business,' he said, then threw the radio to another one of the black-suited men sitting in the van. He grabbed his machine gun with both hands and fired at unit one-five-two.

Bullets cut through the bodywork until one went through a front tyre and the car went into a spin, coming to a stop after slamming into a lamppost at the side of the road. As far as I could see, the driver of the patrol car was unhurt. If he'd wanted to, I'm sure the shooter could have taken us both out with just two shots.

He turned his gun towards me but didn't fire. Instead, he put it down and started to zip up his Kevlar vest, as did the other men in the van. One of them closed the van doors. I looked in my rear view mirror and saw the reason: the tactical aid van was right behind me.

'Welcome to the party,' I said into my radio.

'This is Officer Stewart of the tactical aid unit. Get behind us. We'll take it from here.'

'Okay. Be advised that the van in front contains an innocent witness.'

'We'll do our best,' was the reply. His response wasn't exactly confidence-inspiring but these guys were the best chance of stopping the vans and rescuing the doctor. I knew their primary target was not to save life though; it was to stop the immediate threat to the public. At any cost.

I slowed down to let them past and followed them, expecting them to make their move and run the vans off the road but they stayed in pursuit without taking any action.

I looked around for a clue to why they were stalling but couldn't see a thing.

Why aren't they doing anything?

27
'Come In, Alpha One'

Captain Stein felt the second van start to slow down. 'What the hell are you doing?' he shouted at the driver.

'There's another unit up ahead. It looks like they've put spike strips down.'

'Shit!' Stein exclaimed as he picked up his radio. 'Come in, Alpha One.'

'This is Alpha One. Come in.'

'There's going to be a change of extraction site. Proceed immediately to the Parkway-Freeway intersection.'

'Understood. ETA three minutes.'

'Okay everyone, get ready.'

Captain Stein closed the van doors behind him. All the soldiers in the van zipped up their Kevlar vests, pulled their masks over their faces and checked their weapons. Captain Stein radioed the other van.

'The cops have put spike strips down. Get suited up and secure the doctor.'

'Way ahead of you, Captain,' was the reply, 'Bring it on!'

'Hold on to something, guys', shouted the driver, 'here it comes!'

All four tyres on each van exploded as they bumped over the spike strips. Captain Stein held on for dear life as they skidded to a halt, grinding the metal wheels along the tarmac. He looked out of the window to see the second van flip over onto its side.

No matter what happens, we must save the doctor. Everything depends on it.

Stein's heart was pounding. He had been in worse danger before but no mission had ever been so critical. The Brotherhood had remained underground for centuries but now their fight was out in the open.

The back doors opened and police gunfire rained in, immediately cutting down one of the men. There were two tactical aid vans, each with at least three police sharpshooters who had their sights set firmly on them. Even that goddamn detective was still there, hiding behind his car taking pot shots at them.

Crouching in the van, Captain Stein pulled the pin out of a hand grenade and threw it blindly in the direction of the police vans. He heard a yell of 'Get down!' from outside the van followed by an explosion.

'Everybody out!' he shouted.

The soldiers ran out of the van to find the nearest cover. Another member of their squad was taken down by police gunfire. *Only two men left from this van: the driver and me. Where is he?*

Stein turned round and saw him still sitting in the van, trying to take on the police with a pistol. It was only a matter of time before all rifles were pointing in his direction. Police bullets ripped through the van door like it was tin foil and the driver's head slumped over the smashed glass of the window.

Now he was the only one left from his van who could help the doctor. Captain Stein was crouched behind a parked car, popping his head up every now and then to assess the situation with bullets whistling past his head every time he did.

He heard a call of 'Cover me!' and knew what was going to happen. Bullets rattled through the car he was lying behind and he had no choice but to stay down. He knew the police were advancing on the other van. Now there was nothing he could do. All he could do was lie there and pray for a miracle.

His prayers were answered very quickly. A loud whirring noise overhead got louder and louder and a huge gust of wind threw dust, litter and expelled bullets into the air. It could mean only one thing: Alpha One, a member of The Brotherhood's fleet of gunships, had arrived just in the nick of time.

28
Fatalities

I'd never seen anything like this in my long time on the force. The tactical aid unit had burst the tyres of both vans using spike strips and then taken down three men in no time as they tried to make their escape. The man who shot up unit one-five-two was lying behind a car that was quickly turning into Swiss cheese by all the bullet holes that were puncturing the bodywork.

After the grenade exploded that was thrown from one of the vans, three policemen armed with machine guns had advanced on the van that had flipped onto its side. Everything looked under control until the biggest helicopter I had ever seen appeared overhead. I could see another man in a black suit on board, sitting behind the heaviest-looking machine gun I'd ever seen and began to unload it on everything and everyone that moved.

The tactical aid unit had been within touching distance of the doctor. Now they were dropping like flies. Bullets from the helicopter cannon crunched through their armour. One by one, they all fell to the ground, their blood pouring onto the tarmac. Just as I had frozen in Doctor Forrest's kitchen only a matter of minutes earlier, I hid behind my car and kept completely still again.

When he was certain that there was no one left to shoot at him, the man who was crouched behind the car got up and walked towards the van. I didn't know what to do.

If I stand up and take a shot at him, the soldier in the helicopter will surely take me out then leave with the doctor. If I do nothing, they'll get away with the doctor.

Feeling completely helpless, I told myself there was nothing I could do.

The back doors of the second van opened and three men in black suits got out. They reached in and pulled out a man with glasses wearing a blue shirt and brown slacks who looked to me like he was in his fifties. He wasn't hurt but looked dazed.

Doctor Owen.

The helicopter circled around the scene of devastation and landed on the road. The power from the massive rotor blades created a tornado of dirt and debris. The surviving members of the group ran over to the dead bodies of their colleagues and dragged them into the helicopter, which lifted off and flew far away from the city.

I got up and looked at the remains of my car. It was a complete mess, full of bullet holes from top to bottom. I picked up the radio, which had managed to avoid getting shot to pieces.

'This is Detective Ryder. Come in Dispatch.'

'This is Dispatch. Go ahead.'

'A helicopter is heading south out of the city. Get the chopper to track it. I don't care what it's doing at the moment, get it on the case.'

'The helicopter is currently being refuelled. It will not be ready for another twenty to thirty minutes.'

Goddamn it. Typical penny pinching. We used to have three helicopters but someone sitting in an office cut us down to one so whenever we need it to help with a critical investigation, it's either being refuelled or on the other side of the city looking for a purse snatcher.

'Has the tactical aid unit arrived?'

'Yes,' I said as I surveyed their bloody remains, 'we're going to need about five ambulances at the Parkway-Freeway intersection. The tactical aid unit have suffered severe losses.'

'Can you describe the situation sir? Are there any fatalities?'

'Yes,' I said matter-of-factly, 'most of them.'

29
Surveying The Wreckage

The ambulances were quick to arrive but the paramedics had very little work to do. One member of the tactical aid unit had survived but he was unconscious and bleeding heavily and was rushed off to hospital leaving me to review the remnants of the carnage.

Expelled bullets and shells littered the broken asphalt of the road. The dead bodies were being peeled out of long pools of sticky blood and zipped into body bags. More police were arriving and attempting to divert the heavy traffic in any direction other than towards the wreckage but the rubber-neckers just couldn't help themselves and every few seconds I heard the crunch of another fender bender.

Just when I thought things couldn't get any worse, I saw a swarm of vehicles heading my way that detectives dread the most.

The television crews are here.

The broadcast dishes on the top of their vans wobbled and threatened to fall off as they drew to a halt. The doors all flew open at once and I was faced with a herd of reporters running towards me, brandishing microphones and cameras like a medieval charge towards the enemy. I hate to stereotype people but sometimes when a group of individuals fulfil the same criteria, it's difficult not to.

Bloody reporters. They're all the same.

I recognised several faces. I'm sure they were almost as reluctant to talk to me as I was to deal with them but I was the senior officer on site. Some of my colleagues are best friends with the media and others even make a few pennies on the side by tipping them off but I can't be bothered with them. Unless I decide to use the media to help an investigation, they just get in the way and can even ruin an open and shut case with the wrong type of editorial.

I counted five microphones being thrust into my face and almost in perfect unison I heard a male and female combination of 'What happened here, Detective? How many are dead?'

'No comment.'

'Come on, Detective. You must know who did this? Witnesses said it was a targeted attack on the police by a military outfit.'

'Was it a terrorist attack?'

'No comment.'

'Were you hurt in the attack, detective?'

'Did you fire your weapon?'

'No comment.'

'But detective...'

'Look,' I protested, 'you'll just have to wait for the official statement.' At that moment, my mobile phone rang and I did my best to take the call out of range of the microphones.

'Ryder, what the hell is going on? Why am I watching you on TV?' shouted Captain Nash.

'You won't believe this, Captain,' I said.

'I've got an entire tactical aid unit dead or unconscious. You're the only one there who made it through so tell me what happened.'

'I'm still piecing it together, sir. Our investigation led us to a property belonging to one of the scientists from Mantek. I witnessed a military squad capture the scientist and escape with him in a helicopter. In the process of trying to stop the kidnap, there was a gunfight and the tactical aid unit was neutralised.'

'So who the hell are these people, detective?'

'I don't know yet sir but we still have leads. I'm going back to the property now to pick up Agent Simpson. Something's happening in the city today and we need to move fast.'

'You're damn right, detective. Call me as soon as you have any news.'

'Yes sir, but I'm worried we're going to need more tactical aid before the end of the day.'

'Do your best, detective. You're my best man but try to keep the dead bodies out of the news next time. Right now I'm looking at body bags on TV. It's going to be all over prime time.'

With that, he was gone. As usual, he was more bothered about looking bad on the news than getting the job done. My phone rang again as soon as I had hung up on Captain Nash.

'Hi, Tom. It's Jane. Backup has just arrived and I got your number from Dispatch. Are you okay?'

'A few bruises but I'll live. We're into something bigger than I've ever seen here, Agent Simpson.'

I walked over to the empty van that was lying on its side and looked inside. It was splattered with blood and the metalwork was riddled with bullet holes. On first sight, I could see no equipment left behind other than rifles or any other clues that might help the investigation.

'We still don't know who these guys are,' I continued, 'and they're killing cops for fun.'

'We have to find the scientists,' she said, very assertively, 'the police officer's body has just been picked up and it's being taken to the hospital. We should check it out.'

'You're right. I'll come and pick you up.'

'No, don't worry. I'm going to ride in the ambulance. I'll meet you at the hospital.'

30
Evidence

'Are you gonna be okay in the back there? You can ride up front with me if you want,' said the ambulance driver with a twinkle in his eye.

'I'll be fine, thanks,' said Agent Simpson.

The ambulance driver shrugged and Agent Simpson read his mind as he slammed the doors. *Never mind. Plenty of fish in the sea.*

He's not bad looking I suppose, she thought and laughed to herself, *Their eyes met across a corpse… Not the most romantic beginning.*

The ambulance started to move and she shouted to the driver. 'I'm in a bit of a rush; can you put the siren on?'

'What's up, sweetheart, are you worried he'll die again before we get to the hospital?'

Agent Simpson thought about shooting him with one of her killer stares but decided to change her tactic.

'Please,' she said and batted her eyelids, 'I'll owe you one.'

The ambulance driver smiled. *Sucker.* 'You got it.' And with that, he hit the siren and floored the accelerator. The acceleration made Agent Simpson slide back in her seat.

Now that the driver was less interested in her and more occupied with weaving in and out of the traffic, Agent Simpson turned her attention to the body bag in front of her. She slowly and carefully unzipped the bag to reveal Officer Myers' stony white face and turned his head round to look at his neck. The flesh was torn and the jugular vein had been severed. His face was so white it looked like the blood had completely drained from the top half of his body.

Agent Simpson had one more thing to check. She unzipped the bag further and cast her eyes over the officer's chest. It was full of exit wounds.

As long as there is at least one bullet left in there, all the evidence will disappear very soon.

31
Autopsy Number Two

For the second time in a matter of hours I was leaning over a dead body, only this time it was someone I knew. The naked body of Officer Myers lay on the operating table in front of me. His skin was pale. Most of his blood had soaked into the carpet on Doctor Forrest's landing.

Only a few hours earlier, he had been a high-achieving officer who could have been my next partner. Now the only way he could help me was for his body to give us a clue to aid us in the search for Doctor Owen and his captors.

Doctor Schreiber was closely examining the wound in his neck and Agent Simpson was watching with a concerned look on her face. It crossed my mind that she probably hadn't told me everything she knew about this case and I started to question whether she was purposely hiding something from me.

'Well you're certainly keeping me busy today, Tom,' said Doctor Schreiber in his perpetually upbeat tone, 'This is very interesting. It looks like this wound was caused by an animal bite.'

'An animal bite? That's not possible, Doc. There were no animals in the house,' I said.

'I'm only telling it like I see it, Detective. I've seen a wound like this before.'

'When?' asked Agent Simpson.

'Two years ago, when a young man fell into the lion pen at the zoo. Poor guy.'

'You're saying he was bitten by a lion?' I asked.

Doctor Schreiber shrugged his shoulders. 'It's the only time I've ever seen a wound like this and even then, it was a much bigger bite mark than this. I've found something else weird as well.' He picked up a petri dish containing small silver pellets. 'These are the bullets I pulled out of his back.'

I picked one up with a pair of metal tongs and held it up in the light. It was very shiny and felt heavier than a regular bullet. 'What are they made of? Platinum? Silver?'

'Something like that. Your shooter's obviously not short of a few pennies. Like I said: very weird. I believe it was the gunshots that killed him, not the wound to the neck. Obviously he would have eventually died from blood loss but it was the gunshots that sent him on his way. At least you've made visual contact with the killers.'

'Great. All I've got to do is find them, stop them blowing my brains out, arrest them and bring back the doctor. Simple as that, eh?' *Not a hint of sarcasm in my voice as I rolled my eyes.*

I turned to Agent Simpson. 'Why are you so interested in all of this? Shouldn't you be back at Mantek helping to tidy up?'

She fired a look at me that told me I was over-stepping the mark.

'Sorry,' I conceded, 'it's been a long day. I should have been at home tucked up in bed today. Instead, here we are.'

'Forget it,' she said, 'This isn't exactly my idea of a good time either but the reason I'm here is the same reason you're here. The whole case depends on us finding Doctor Owen. You have to find him to solve the murder. I have to find him to allow him to continue his work.'

Doctor Schreiber piped up. 'Look, I've still got some work to do here so why don't you go and wait outside?'

This was our best lead and we had to just sit outside and wait for Doctor Schreiber to finish cutting him up. My face must have betrayed my feelings because the doctor commented immediately after looking me in the eye.

'Okay Detective, if you want to stay here and help, be my guest but like you say, it's been a long day. I think you can be forgiven for taking a few minutes off. I promise to tell you as soon as I find out anything at all.'

He's got a point, I thought.

'Sounds good to me,' I said, relaxing slightly and turned to Agent Simpson, realising how long it had been since I'd eaten. 'Can I buy you dinner?'

She nodded with a smile.

32
Dinner For Two

'Sorry it's not a candle-lit dinner for two,' I said as we arrived at the hot dog stand around the corner from the hospital. The sun was lower in the sky and the humidity was starting to subside.

'That's okay,' she said, 'I haven't eaten since breakfast and this is much better than the hospital canteen.'

'Once we find the doctor and solve the murders, we'll hit the town,' I said speculatively.

'Sounds good to me,' she said. I wasn't expecting her to reciprocate. I hoped she meant it.

I ordered and paid for two hot dogs: mustard and onions for me, ketchup and no onions for her. I took a bite and hoped it would stop the incessant rumbling in my stomach. I took the last bite of my hot dog and ordered a second before I'd finished off the first.

'Pretty hungry, huh?' she noticed.

'I haven't eaten all day either,' I said, 'Actually, I never really eat anything resembling food. If I have one more, it'll be my first three course dinner in years.' Agent Simpson laughed at that, which I wasn't expecting. I had been hoping it would raise a smile though.

'Someone needs to sort his life out, doesn't he? Forgive me for being presumptuous but I'm guessing you're not married. Am I right?' Agent Simpson asked as she took a bite out of her hot dog. A spot of ketchup stuck in the corner of her mouth. Before I could decide whether to tell her or not, she licked it off. I must have stared at her for a second too long.

'Well, am I right?' she asked again.

'What makes you say that?' I asked sarcastically. She smiled again. *God knows how, but I might actually be close to being charming here.*

'I was married,' I said.

'What happened?'

I decided to tell her. 'She's dead.'

Her face was suddenly filled with the look I always see when someone finds out about Sarah, a mixture of sympathy and wishing they'd never brought up the subject in the first place. Before she could say anything, I told her not to worry.

'It was years ago. I'm over it now,' I lied, 'what about you?'

'Never married. I've had a few near misses but I've got too much going on in my life. I don't think I've got room for a man.'

'A career woman, huh? Don't you want kids? Part of me wants to have kids but another part of me knows that if I can't even take good care of myself, the kids wouldn't have a chance.'

'I'm sure it'll happen one day,' she said, 'there's plenty of time left for both of us.'

My mind turned to the case. 'So what the hell are we going to do? How can we compete with those guys today? You know more about this case than I do. Have you got any idea who they were?'

'No idea at all,' she replied almost instantly. She was a bit too quick to answer. I tried to push my suspicions to the back of my mind. 'Whoever they are, they're obviously well funded.'

'And well trained. I thought they were military until they started killing cops. The problem now is that we've got nothing to go on. We've hit a dead end.'

'Don't lose heart. We'll get a break. Silver bullets, remember? There can't be many places that make silver bullets in this area. And we've still got Doctor Forrest to find.'

'The best lead we've got is the doctor's wife but now that he's been taken again, it's unlikely that she'll be able to give us anything that will lead us to him now. I've been doing this for years but I still hate all the waiting around.'

'Because you like to be in control? You don't want to have to depend on other people,' she speculated.

I looked at her.

'Takes one to know one,' she said and we both smiled.

We both leaned against the wall outside the hospital and shared a moment of peace, lost in our own thoughts as we finished our hot dogs. A cool breeze blew past us as the sun went down.

33
Successful Return

Commander North stood on the front steps of Hartley House, watching the sun go down behind the mountains in the distance. It had been a hard day but The Brotherhood had prevailed. They had successfully fought off meddling cops and one of *them* to rescue Doctor Owen and allow him to continue his noble work.

Doctor Forrest was still missing though. No one in the outside world had heard anything from him for several days, which meant that either he was dead or *they* were holding him captive for another reason. Commander North didn't know which option was preferable for The Brotherhood or the doctor himself.

A squad of soldiers ran out of the door behind the commander and down the steps to a large clearing adjoining the drive in front of the house. They all checked their weapons and clicked the safety catches. They had to be prepared for every eventuality. Everyone was confident that the approaching helicopter carried Doctor Owen, Captain Stein and the surviving members of their squad but until they checked who was on board, they wouldn't know for sure.

The helicopter glided over the grounds and touched down without incident. The soldiers lowered their weapons when they saw the passengers getting out of the helicopter and proceeding as expected. Most of the soldiers aboard the helicopter were bandaged in some way and did not appear to be seriously harmed but there should have been a few more of them.

A pair of soldiers escorted Doctor Owen, who was moving rather gingerly, up the front steps and into Hartley House. Commander North approached Captain Stein as he marched up the steps. They saluted each other as they met.

'Congratulations,' said Commander North, 'I see the doctor has arrived in one piece.'

'That's correct sir, but we sustained losses during the extraction,' said Captain Stein as he watched the soldiers start to unload the dead bodies from the helicopter.

Commander North didn't bat an eyelid. 'They were acceptable losses and you recovered the bodies,' was his heartless reply, 'the mission was completed successfully. How is the doctor?'

'A bit shaken up but he'll be okay. He didn't say much on the flight over from the city.'

'Does he have enough equipment to continue his work?'

'Yes,' said Captain Stein, 'we have the basics and I believe there are enough samples here to allow him to catch up on the time he has lost in the last few days.'

'Good. After the destruction of the lab last night, I expect him to be back on track by this time tomorrow. I'm going to return to regional HQ tonight once the helicopter has been refuelled so I'll be in touch tomorrow. I expect you to present results the next time we see speak.'

'Yes sir,' said Captain Stein as they saluted each other before parting company.

34
Home Time

Doctor Schreiber sighed and put his instruments down. He decided to call it quits for the night. He had searched every inch of Officer Myers' body and did not find anything of note in addition to the expensive bullet wounds and the 'animal' bite.

It was the most unorthodox combination of wounds he had ever seen. Coupled with the bodies from the Mantek attack, it had been a very strange and hectic day.

Someone's very busy out there. How many more are on the hit list? How many more times will I be standing over a body with Detective Ryder and his new partner in the next few days?

Well, that might not be too bad, he thought. Agent Simpson was certainly very easy on the eye but she had been asking questions that gave him the feeling that she knew more about the day's events than she was letting on.

His observations kept leading him towards a conclusion that he was fighting very hard to entertain. He knew it was nonsensical but what other possible explanation could there be?

It can't be. I'm definitely not going to mention it to Detective Ryder. He'd have me committed.

Doctor Schreiber threw a plastic sheet over the body of Officer Myers and washed his hands in the sink. He packed away his instruments and looked at his watch.

Oh my God, is it really that late?

He had lost track of time. Doctor Schreiber enjoyed his work and minutes could turn into hours very quickly. He knew he should find Detective Ryder and tell him that he hadn't found anything else but he was now in a rush to get home.

He heard the beep of his mobile phone from his bag in the corner of the room and he knew what the message would say before he checked it. His wife Lucy would not be happy. No doubt she was informing him that his dinner was either cold or in the dog. Brandy, their beloved Chihuahua, was probably the best-fed dog in the whole city.

Doctor Schreiber threw his jacket on and flicked the lights off on his way out of the door. In his haste to leave the lab, he didn't notice the plastic sheet covering the body of Officer Myers start to twitch.

35
The Penny Drops

Agent Simpson and I stood in silence. I opened a can of Coke, no Diet crap for me, took a big gulp and my thoughts turned to work again.

'We'd better get back in there,' said Agent Simpson as she looked at her watch, 'see if the doctor needs any help.'

'Don't worry,' I said, 'he'll come out here and tell us as soon as he finds anything.' Agent Simpson looked like she wanted to protest but sat back down on the wall.

'What about the work Doctor Owen and Doctor Forrest were doing?' I asked, 'Can you tell me more about it? You must know more than you've told me so far.'

'As I said, he was working on the treatment for a disease. He has been working on it for years and years. The World Health Organisation has been funding their research.'

'Why is this treatment so important? What are the symptoms of the disease?'

'It's a blood disorder that consumes the whole body. Once you have the disease; you stop being yourself.'

I'm no doctor, but that explanation sounds deliberately vague even to me.

'It has a psychological effect?'

'Yes. Both psychological and physiological.'

It was obvious I would have to work very hard to get specific details from her.

'Does it have a name?'

Agent Simpson didn't get the chance to answer my question. Not ten feet away from us, a woman was staring down the alley next to the hospital, screaming at the top of her lungs. She had a look of complete horror on her face.

I drew my gun and ran over to her. She didn't move or even register my presence. She just kept staring directly ahead. I followed her gaze down the alley and couldn't believe what I saw.

Surely this isn't possible? What the hell is going on?

Hiding in the shadows was a naked man, crouched over a homeless man sitting against the wall, surrounded by dirty plastic bags that were now awash with his blood. The homeless man was struggling, waving his hands around and trying to escape the grip of his attacker, who was chewing on his neck.

'Hey! Let him go or I'll be forced to shoot you!' I shouted.

The naked man looked up at me with blood covering his mouth. His eyes were vacant and he looked lost. Then it hit me who this man was.

Officer Myers.

He stood up and started to approach me. I pointed my gun at him and told him not to move but he kept coming.

'Don't make me shoot you!' I shouted. Officer Myers stopped moving and looked up to the top of the high walls of the hospital.

He jumped into the air; higher than I thought was humanly possible. Then he performed gravity-defying leaps from one wall to another and onto the top of the hospital. I ran round the side of the building, hoping to catch a glimpse of him but he had gone.

I walked back to meet Agent Simpson, who didn't look as shocked as I undoubtedly did. For some reason, I wasn't surprised.

Then the penny dropped.

Why didn't I think of this before?

The neck wound, the silver bullets, the blood disorder and Officer Myers coming back to life all added up to one thing. Something terrible that I didn't want to believe.

I was overcome with a wave of emotion, which felt like the world was shifting around me. This was a dream. A nightmare.

I walked right up to her and shouted in her face. 'Okay Agent Simpson, it's time to come clean. What aren't you telling me about this blood disorder?'

'What do you mean?'

'Officer Myers just turned into a fucking vampire! Now tell me what's going on!'

36
Marcus And Roxy

Marcus Verrico was lying in complete darkness, meditating on his position in the world. It was nine o'clock in the evening and the sun had just set. If he had opened the blackout blinds and let the sunlight in earlier in the day, he would have died within a matter of minutes. He suffered from a blood disorder that had several side effects, one of which made his skin hypersensitive to the ultraviolet rays from the sun.

He was a vampire.

In just over five hundred years he had worked his way up to the leader of a clan. Hundreds of his brothers and sisters were under his command and looked to him for guidance in their undead lives. Marcus and the other clan leaders answered to only one man: the Lord Chancellor. It was his ambition to one day assume the role of Lord Chancellor.

Marcus already had the favour of the Lord Chancellor and he knew that by finding Doctor Owen, he would have a good chance of working with him more closely. The Lord Chancellor already had an apprentice though. The apprentice was the deputy Lord Chancellor; the person who would take over leadership of the global vampire community should anything happen to their leader.

The deputy, Luca Salazar, supposedly commanded a large number of clans, including Marcus' but Marcus refused to consider him a figure of authority. The deputy was a brown-nose who had slimed his way to the top. He had only been a vampire for fifty years but had friends in high places.

One day he'll get what's coming to him, Marcus thought to himself. *Maybe that day will be a lot sooner than he thinks.*

The door to his room opened and in walked Roxy, his loyal assistant. Dressed from head to toe in black combat gear, she was not a woman to be messed with. As assistant to the leader, she was more heavily armed than other members of the clan. She carried two swords on her back, one with a solid steel blade, the other silver-plated. Roxy was one of the few members of the vampire community with a licence to kill her brothers and sisters.

Marcus and Roxy had worked together for almost three hundred years. They had circled the globe together many times, moving from clan to clan, setting the standards for vampires to live by. They had been instrumental in helping the vampire community gain influence in high places. The seeds of corruption and influence they had sown all those years ago allowed their brothers and sisters to live in the freedom they now enjoyed.

They both owed each other their lives. They had made a pact to stick together forever and swore that whoever was given an opportunity would take the other forward with them. As it turned out, Marcus had moved up the ladder quicker than Roxy but she didn't care. She respected him and lived to serve her great leader. In her eyes, Marcus was born to lead their brothers and sisters to glory.

Marcus awoke immediately and sat up straight.

'Forgive me for waking you, my master,' Roxy said in her calm, soothing voice, 'but I have important news.'

'I understand. What is it?'

'*They* have the doctor,' she said.

'The Brotherhood?'

'Yes, sir.'

The doctor had been captured and lost on Marcus' watch. He had been quick to report back to the deputy Lord Chancellor on the capture but the loss of their precious hostage would have to be dealt with quickly. If they could get him back before the news filtered up to the deputy then Marcus would stay in the favour of the Lord Chancellor.

There were many clan leaders waiting for Marcus to put a foot wrong so they could take the opportunity to side-step him to the top.

'And what of our brother who was guarding the doctor?'

'Dead.'

Marcus closed his eyes for a second and shook his head. 'Get the doctor back at all costs. Tonight.'

'Yes sir.'

37
'Let's Talk'

'I think you're being a bit over-dramatic,' Agent Simpson said in a considerably calmer tone than mine.

'Over-dramatic?' I shouted, even louder this time.

Agent Simpson stayed calm, probably hoping it would rub off on me. 'This isn't the place. Let's talk in the car.'

We got into the car and I slammed the door. It was a pool car, a replacement for my old car that had been impounded as evidence of the battle that afternoon. I'm not sure what point I was trying to prove by slamming the door but I needed to vent somehow. I wasn't even sure what I was venting. Anger? Shock? A feeling of complete disillusionment and helplessness?

I picked up the radio. 'Dispatch, this is Detective Ryder. Make sure all units are on the lookout for Officer Myers. He used to be dead but now he's naked and running round the streets near the hospital, eating homeless guys.'

'This is Dispatch. Please can you repeat that, Detective Ryder?'

'You heard,' I said and threw the radio onto the dashboard. I turned to Agent Simpson. 'Now let's talk.'

She sighed. 'Where do you want to me start?'

'You're the vampire expert,' I exclaimed, 'tell me everything. Where do they come from? What do they want? How can we kill them?'

She took a deep breath, like she was about to recite a story she had told a hundred times before. 'As far as we know, vampires have always been a part of the human community. There is documented evidence of their existence going back as far as man has been able to put ink to paper.

'There have always been two theories for their existence: either the vampires themselves are a species of their own that has mutated from mankind or that their behaviour is caused by a disorder of the blood and they are still human deep down.'

'So the World Health Organisation have discovered that it's a blood disorder?' I asked in a lower tone of voice.

'No, not exactly. Doctor Owen has been working with samples of vampire blood. He and many scientists before him have discovered that there are certain ways of treating the blood to cause a chemical reaction. Some treatments could eventually be used to remove the symptoms and the other treatments will be used to kill vampires in a more effective way than silver bullets.'

'It is true that humans can inherit some of a vampire's attributes when he or she is bitten. The World Health Organisation also suspects there is a core of pure blood vampires who are the direct descendants of the very first vampires, just as we are the direct descendants of the first human beings that evolved from the apes.'

At first I was surprised this was such a big secret. How could there be a worldwide vampire community without it being obvious to everyone?

Then I realised what would happen if this information got out. If the six billion human beings on this Earth suddenly realised they weren't at the top of the food chain there would be complete panic.

I wanted to ask her why she hadn't come clean with me from the beginning. *Why didn't she just tell me about all this when we met this morning?*

I already knew the answer to that question as well. I wouldn't have believed her for one second and I would have tried to have her committed.

'I can understand why you want to keep the existence of vampires secret from everyone but what about the vampire community? Outside of the movies, this is the first I've heard about them. How do they keep such a low profile?'

'Compared with the human race, their community is very small. They have a presence in most major cities in the world but they keep their numbers under control. They need to feed regularly and big cities are easy places to sweep missing people under the carpet. They're not stupid though. They know that if they were to launch an attack on a large group of humans, it would attract attention, get in the papers and on the news and life would change for everyone.

'Once people get over the initial panic and get used to their new place in the world, they always come to realise that vampires aren't actually that hard to kill.'

Now we were getting to the interesting part. 'How can we kill them?'

'Forget what you know about garlic and crucifixes, that's straight out of the movies. Silver and ultraviolet light are the best weapons against them. The blood of a vampire reacts in different ways to external influences than human blood.

'After an hour or so in direct sunlight without sunscreen, you and I would get pretty bad sunburn. The vampires' skin is hypersensitive to UV light so they get the same kind of sunburn after just a few minutes or even seconds in some cases.'

'So vampires are all creatures of the night, like in the movies?' I asked, trying to relate what I thought I knew.

'Not at all. As long as they stay out of direct exposure to the sun, they can carry on as normal. Remember, it's not the light itself that harms them, it's the UV rays. If you sit in a car in the height of summer, your skin won't burn because the glass in the windows absorbs most of the UV rays. They use similar techniques to operate in daylight hours. There's a very good chance you run into vampires in your daily life. They've had centuries to practice being incognito.'

It would be very difficult to forget what movies had taught me. These vampires weren't demons from hell sent here to take our souls; they were unfortunate people that had contracted a terrible disease. Or that was the theory anyway.

Agent Simpson continued. 'Doctor Owen has discovered that silver reacts with a compound in vampire blood to produce an acid that burns their bodies from the inside. The acid is so strong that it breaks down all tissue and bone. Once a vampire absorbs a silver bullet, it only takes a few seconds for the whole body to decompose.'

'That's why there were burns marks on the wall in the house where Officer Myers was killed,' I concluded, 'The doctor was being held there by vampires, wasn't he? The guys who snatched the doctor must have had silver bullets in their guns. Who are they?'

'They call themselves The Brotherhood. They are a group who devote their lives to the protection of the human race.'

All day long I had known she knew who they were. 'But they killed policemen today.'

'They operate outside the law and at times they take extreme action for the good of mankind. The vampires must have picked up Doctor Owen last night. With your help, The Brotherhood tracked him down and rescued him.'

'With my help? That's the real reason you're working with me today, isn't it? You're one of them and you wanted the inside scoop.'

She nodded in agreement. 'I'm afraid so, detective. I wanted to tell you but I feel that the information I am sharing with you is on a need to know basis. Only now do you need to know.'

I thought she was right but I didn't tell Agent Simpson that I agreed with her.

'Do you think they have Doctor Forrest as well?' I asked.

'We should assume they have him, yes.'

'So it must have been the vampires that blew up the Mantek lab,' I said, 'they discovered Doctor Owen was working on the treatment and took action against him.'

Agent Simpson nodded in agreement.

Another thought occurred to me. 'But if the vampires destroyed the lab, all of his work and killed his assistant, why didn't they kill the doctor?'

'I'm afraid I don't have the answer to that,' said Agent Simpson. Given my experience of working with her so far, I didn't know whether to believe her or not.

38
Another Strategy

Marcus Verrico was sitting in his office in silence, quietly contemplating the days ahead. Everyone from the vampires to The Brotherhood had been waiting in anticipation for the wheels to be set in motion. Now that everything had begun, there was no stopping either group.

He knew all about the plans of The Brotherhood. They had their men on the inside and The Brotherhood were always so surprised when Marcus and his clan second-guessed them. For hundreds of years Marcus had kept one step ahead and now the first part of his plan was almost complete. He picked up a stack of scientific papers and thumbed through them.

Positive results. Becoming more encouraging as the days passed. *It helps to have the best men on your side.*

Some of his allies within the other clans had already been in touch to offer their services and offer encouragement. He declined their offers for now but warned them that their help would be needed very soon. Looking at the results again, he knew the next step was only days away.

No more hiding in the shadows. No more balance between the ancient enemies. It is time to take control and I will be the one to lead my brothers and sisters.

There was a problem though. It was only a matter of time before *he* got in touch and with that thought, the phone on his desk started to ring.

He reluctantly answered it, knowing exactly who the caller would be. The voice on the other end grated on him from the first word.

'Good evening, Marcus,' lisped Luca Salazar, the deputy Lord Chancellor, 'how are you today?'

'Great thanks,' Marcus replied. *Get to the point, asshole*, he thought. 'What can I do for you, Luca?'

'I thought I would call in advance to advise you of our imminent arrival.'

Marcus sat upright in his chair. 'The Lord Chancellor is coming here?' he asked.

There was a pause for a few seconds before Salazar replied. Marcus could tell that Salazar was enjoying this opportunity to make him sweat. 'No, I'm going to be visiting later tonight. The Lord Chancellor has asked me to advise you on the tactics for recovering the doctor and his work, and to provide hands-on assistance if necessary.'

He hated pussyfooting around and decided to get right to the point. 'So you're coming here to tell me how to run my clan?' Marcus asked.

'Like I said, I've been asked to provide help wherever I can. It certainly looks like you need the help, unless you've already managed to recover the doctor?'

That son of a bitch. He knows we haven't got the doctor.

'Not yet, but we're closing in,' said Marcus, 'We know where the doctor is being held and we have already formulated our strategy. There's really no need for you to come here.'

'I beg to differ, Marcus,' said Salazar, 'If you've already formulated your strategy then I'd like to be there when the doctor is returned to us. It is a long time since there was an operation of this importance. I long to see a well-trained squad in action. I shall look forward to seeing you in approximately three hours.'

Marcus didn't have the chance to protest any further before Salazar hung up on him. He hated that slimy bastard. Salazar knew Marcus was a threat to his deputyship and was doing all he could to undermine his authority.

If they failed to return Doctor Owen to the vampires, it would be the end of him. Unless he came up with a different plan of course.

Marcus Verrico rubbed the short stubble on his chin and started to formulate another strategy.

39
Scouring The Streets

Matthew Duffy was one hundred and forty seven years old. He hadn't felt the heat of the sun on his face since the early years of the twentieth century and had feasted on thousands of people since his rebirth over one hundred years ago.

He was a member of the scout team who scoured the city streets every night, looking for potential future bothers and sisters or for new brothers and sisters who may have been reborn without the knowledge of the clan. It was important for all vampires to be accounted for and successfully integrated into the community.

The Alsatian sitting on the back seat was his trusty helper, Goldie. Dogs could sniff out a vampire at a hundred paces, even from a moving vehicle.

Goldie had been Matthew's companion for many years and had saved his undead life so many times he had lost count.

That was why Matthew spoiled him. The dogs were only supposed to feed on the bones of dead humans but every time he made a kill, Matthew would give Goldie a juicy piece of flesh to get his fangs into.

Scout work had been very uneventful over the past few weeks. The clan had been busy preparing for the battle they knew was coming. Once it was all over and they were victorious, they would all hit the streets of this city and many others and their numbers would grow exponentially.

Matthew had heard that there had been some excitement that day at some doctor's house so there was a possibility that someone had been bitten and reborn at sundown. The scout team had many members so the chance of him being the one to find the new recruit was very slim.

He drove around for a little while without seeing or hearing anything out of the ordinary. When he was about to take a break after driving past the hospital, he heard a scream from outside. His sixth sense told him there was a friend nearby.

Matthew stopped the car and rolled down the window. Almost immediately, Goldie started to bark.

40
Fresh Meat

The Paparazzi bar and nightclub is one of the most exclusive nightspots in the city. Even though the place was practically empty inside, a long queue was building on the street outside. It's one of those places that lets the punters freeze outside for hours to let passers-by know that it's an exclusive joint and then charge a fortune behind the bar to make up for lost time when they finally let them in.

This night was no exception. A lucky few had managed to get past the bouncers and were enjoying the relative ease of getting served at the bar. Two people had a little more perseverance.

Josh Daniels and Jimmy Foster had a few drinks in Paparazzi after work and didn't leave, even when the bar was cleared for half an hour so the staff could rearrange the furniture for the night. They didn't leave because the night staff didn't think to check the toilets for two young men hiding in the cubicles who had been thrown out the night before. And the night before that.

The nightclub is popular with the city's celebrities and Josh and Jimmy can't help themselves when there are local seventeen year-old female soap opera and singing stars drinking in the same venue as them. Needless to say their success rate with these girls was negligible but that didn't stop them wasting their minimum-wage packets out on the prowl every night.

Unfortunately for them, they were a little too eager on this night and emerged from the toilets before a significant crowd had built up in the bar. It wasn't long before the security staff found them and escorted them to the back door by their collars, a route that had become all too familiar to them.

The rear entrance of the nightclub can be found down a back alley, well hidden from the crowds both inside and outside. It also has the added bonus of being a mobile phone black spot where no network can provide adequate coverage.

This is where the security staff can comfortably beat up a couple of unpopular clients then throw them in the dumpsters and call the police to come and pick them up without causing any unwanted attention, which is exactly what happened to Josh and Jimmy.

A bag of rubbish burst as Josh's head hit it at high speed and he found himself face-down in chicken bones and cold baked beans. When Jimmy's head hit the bags in the second dumpster, they didn't burst. The cans and broken bottles had already punctured the bags long ago. Blood was already pouring down his face from the cuts around his eyes so the broken bottles didn't make that much difference to his appearance.

The extra cuts on Jimmy's face didn't make much difference to the vampire that used to be called Officer Myers either. He had already locked onto the scent of fresh blood from two streets away and was frantically leaping from rooftop to rooftop in search of the second feed of his new life.

Jimmy was moaning to Josh about their rotten luck with the Nazi doormen when Officer Myers landed in his dumpster with a thud.

'Hey, what was that?' he exclaimed as he noticed the naked, blood-soaked body next to him. He didn't get a chance to utter another audible word because Officer Myers' razor sharp canine teeth ripped a hole in Jimmy's neck and removed his larynx in one bite. Officer Myers spat the chunk of flesh out of his mouth and began to feed on Jimmy's warm blood as it flowed from his body.

Josh heard Jimmy's scream and realised something was wrong. He clambered out of the dumpster and wobbled over, his legs still not responding properly after the beating he had taken to his head.

Hearing a kind of squelchy-slurping noise from inside, Josh very slowly lifted himself up and peered into the dumpster to see a naked man sucking blood out of his best friend's neck.

'What the…' he started and Officer Myers turned around. His whole body was completely white and his eyes were bloodshot. Blood dripped out of his mouth and down his chin, onto his chest. As he licked his lips, Josh noticed his canine teeth were a lot longer than usual. Sort of like a vampire's…

'No way! No fucking way!'

41
'I'm Here To Help You'

Officer Benson had already dealt with two drunk and disorderlies since his shift had started four hours earlier. One of them went home with a friend and the other was locked up in a drying-out cell at the police station. That was about normal for this time of night but after the witching hour he knew he'd have to call for backup on every call. Once the people of this city have a few drinks in them they can get very rowdy and after five years on the night shift, Officer Benson had the scars to prove it.

He picked up his third call of the night, which sounded like more of the same. An anonymous call came from the Paparazzi nightclub, saying that two young men had barged their way into the club and proceeded to knock hell out of each other.

Officer Benson suspected this wasn't the truth. He had dealt with the security staff at Paparazzi before and knew they liked to teach wrongdoers a lesson but the punishment was always a little too harsh for the crime. The police department happily turned a blind eye to this kind of behaviour, as long as no one was seriously injured and the victims learned their lesson.

Officer Benson agreed with this philosophy. There had been endless 'stop drinking' campaigns and non-stop propaganda to point out the ills of alcohol consumption but the authorities were starting to realise that all people want to do when they finish their shifts is go out, get drunk and act like idiots.

It's twenty-first century human nature.

As he turned his patrol car round the corner past the hospital, Officer Benson considered going into the club but thought he'd check the usual dropping off point for people who've been ejected: the dumpsters in the alley round the back.

He stopped his car and got out, seeing Josh looking into one of the dumpsters. As he unclipped his handcuffs, Officer Benson shouted to the young man, 'Are you okay, son? What have you been up to tonight?'

Josh didn't move an inch. As he approached the dumpster, Officer Benson noticed that the young man looked very scared. He had bruises and scratches on his blood-drained face. No doubt he was coming to terms with the beating he had just received. Officer Benson tried to offer words of encouragement. 'Don't worry, son. The bruises will heal. You'll feel a lot better in the morning.'

Not two seconds later, the blood-soaked naked body of Officer Myers leapt out of the dumpster, grabbed the young man by the neck and threw him against the wall. Josh slumped to the ground, completely still.

Officer Benson drew his gun and pointed it at the naked man. Like everyone else who had seen Officer Myers since his rebirth, he couldn't believe his eyes.

Blood was pouring down his face, coating his chest.

His eyes looked like they were staring straight through him.

His canine teeth were unnaturally long.

Am I looking at a real life vampire? I can't be! More importantly, will the bullets in my gun take it down?

Before he had a chance to try and deal with this freak of nature, he heard an engine roaring behind him. He spun round to see a pair of bright lights moving towards him at high speed. He jumped out of the way and hit the ground just as the car stopped where he had been standing. Officer Myers was face to face with a hubcap. He breathed a sigh of relief to be alive.

Looking up, he saw a dog's head hanging out of the back window, barking like mad. It was all so unreal, everything appeared to happen in slow motion. A tall, very pale man got out of the car and extended a hand to Officer Myers.

'I'm here to help you. Get in the car and I'll take you to safety,' he said in a soft yet purposeful voice.

Very slowly, Officer Myers shuffled towards the tall man, who put an arm round him and guided him into the back seat of the car, next to the dog which had stopped barking.

The tall man got back into the driver's seat and the car screeched out of the alley. Officer Benson got to his feet and ran to pick up the radio from his patrol car.

I definitely need backup on this call.

42

Asleep At Last

I thought I'd had it rough that morning. I had been overworked and crying out for a decent night's sleep.

But compared with what was to come, it was nothing.

Now I was sitting in my car with a vampire hunter having found out there had been a war going on between humans and vampires since the beginning of time. Agent Simpson explained a lot to me but I knew she had only scratched the surface. I would have given anything to go back to this morning and avoid this case.

There wasn't any time for it all to sink in before we had to hit the road again. The radio fizzed into life.

'This is unit one-four-three calling for backup. I'm in pursuit of a dark blue Toyota heading past the hospital. The driver is to be considered dangerous and the passenger has attacked two men. Both are in a critical condition.'

I immediately picked it up. 'Unit one-four-three, this is Detective Ryder. Was the attacker naked?'

'That's right, Detective.'

Agent Simpson pointed to a police car speeding down the road past the hospital. 'Look, that must be him.'

'We've spotted you and we're on our way. Do not attempt to engage the suspects until we are with you.'

Before long we had caught up with unit one-four-three, which was tailing a dark blue Toyota. I put the portable siren on the roof of my car but Agent Simpson stopped me from turning it on.

'Wait,' she said, 'before you engage them, take this.' She reached into her jacket and pulled out a gun. A black revolver that looked like it had never been used.

'I've got a gun,' I said.

'Your gun's useless against them, remember? This one's loaded with silver bullets.' She passed the gun to me. It was a six-shooter so I told myself I'd better not waste the bullets.

'Unit one-four-three,' I said into the radio, 'you take the right, I'll take the left. Hit your siren and we'll try and pull these guys over.'

Unit one-four-three turned his siren on and so did I. We flanked the car in front in an effort to get it to stop. I wasn't expecting the driver to pull over so I wasn't surprised when he spun the steering wheel and smashed into the patrol car.

I drew my regular gun and tried to shoot out the tyres with two shots but missed with both. The driver then slammed his car into mine and I gripped the wheel hard with two hands to regain control.

Officer Myers then launched himself through the back windscreen of the car in front. The naked vampire flew through the air and landed on the bonnet of my car with a loud thud. I hit the brakes, hoping that Officer Myers would turn into road kill but he somehow managed to cling on.

I picked up Agent Simpson's gun, leaned out of the window and fired two shots in the direction of the vampire but missed. The other car slammed into mine again and I nearly dropped the gun.

I fired another shot at the front tyre, knowing I was wasting a silver bullet but I didn't have time to swap guns. Luckily, this bullet went to good use. The tyre burst and the Toyota swerved and spun to a halt. Now I only had three shots left. I fired another one at Officer Myers but missed again.

A bus pulled out in front of me at an intersection and I had to drop the gun on my lap to hit the brakes and slide the car out of the way. As the car spun across the road, narrowly missing the bus, Officer Myers crawled up the bonnet and punched through the windscreen. The glass shattered onto us and he grabbed me by the neck, pulling me out of my seat.

Agent Simpson pulled on the handbrake. The car came to a halt with me being held in the air on the bonnet. I punched Officer Myers' head and torso but nothing could stop him pulling me in close and sinking his teeth into my neck.

I screamed in complete agony. The pain was unlike anything I had ever felt before. All I could hear were deafening sucking noises in my left ear as the vampire lapped up the blood that was draining from my body.

I heard a gunshot and the vampire lost its grip. I hit the bonnet and looked up to see dust pouring from a wound in his chest. More and more dust poured onto me as the wound grew larger and larger. Officer

Myers' body was dissolving in front of me and blowing away in the summer breeze.

His body disappeared into the air and I was left lying on the bonnet of my car with the life in me leaking out of a gaping wound in my neck.

For the first time in forty-eight hours, I slipped into unconsciousness.

Part Two

Twilight

43
Disobeying Orders

The last speck of dust flew away into the night's sky, leaving Detective Ryder alone on the bonnet of the car. Agent Simpson's hands were shaking as she lowered her gun. She hadn't been quick enough to save Detective Ryder from being bitten.

As she stepped out of the car, her thoughts turned to the vampire in the car they ran off the road. She saw Officer Benson on the other side of the road, checking over an empty car.

Damn it, we've let the other one escape.

With no immediate leads and a dying cop in front of her, she knew she had to do something she swore she would never do. Detective Ryder had passed out but the blood hadn't stopped pouring from his neck. She took off her jacket and tied it round his neck, keeping as much pressure on the wound as possible without choking him.

Within seconds, her dark grey jacket had turned a deep shade of red. Agent Simpson dragged Detective Ryder's limp body into the back seat of the car, just as Officer Benson ran across the road to her.

'Oh my God,' he said as he saw the body of Detective Ryder, 'I'll call for an ambulance.'

'No,' she said abruptly, 'it's okay, I'll take him to the hospital. It's not far from here.'

Without waiting to hear a reply, Officer Simpson hit the accelerator and screeched away in the opposite direction to the hospital.

She headed out of the city and into the countryside. What she was about to do went against her orders: never help a victim and never bring a victim to an outpost of The Brotherhood. It didn't take long for her to reach her destination: Hartley House.

She drove the pale, blood-soaked body of Detective Ryder up the long drive to the front steps of Hartley House, where Captain Stein and a team of soldiers were waiting with their rifles pointed at the car. She knew the security team would have alerted Captain Stein to her arrival as soon as she was within a mile of the outpost.

'What the hell are you doing, Agent Simpson?' Captain Stein demanded, as Agent Simpson dragged Detective Ryder out of the car on to the gravel drive.

'Get a stretcher. We have to get him inside.'

'He's been bitten, hasn't he? You know the rules: shoot him in the head now.'

'No! Screw the rules. You wouldn't have the doctor if it wasn't for this man. You owe it to him. We all owe it to him!'

'This is the guy who tried to run us off the road. He was a problem when he was human, now he's a vampire and you know we have to kill him.' He flicked the safety catch on his rifle and moved towards Detective Ryder.

In a flash, Agent Simpson jumped up, drew her gun and held it against Captain Stein's head. The soldiers on the steps immediately changed their aim and Agent Simpson found herself at the wrong end of ten rifles. Her heart was pumping like she'd just run a marathon and she was terrified on the inside but on the outside she was determined to stay as cool and collected as always.

I'm in control here, not them, she kept repeating over and over to herself.

'Get the doctor and treat this man,' she ordered, 'or I'll unload in your head.'

'You know you won't last much longer than me. As soon as you pull that trigger, you're dead.'

'I don't care. This man can be saved and we have to help him. Get the doctor. That's an order, soldier.' She pushed the gun hard against Captain Stein's head. After a few seconds' thought, Captain Stein relented.

'Okay, okay. You win.' He waved an arm to the soldiers and they lowered their rifles. 'Get a stretcher and send the doctor to the medical room.' Two soldiers ran into Hartley House to carry out the orders.

'You can lower your gun now, Agent Simpson,' he said. She felt her hand shaking as she did so and cursed herself for showing weakness. 'They'll be on their way here right now. They always know where the new bloodsuckers are.'

'We have to assume they know you've got the doctor. They're already on their way here anyway.'

'You're right,' said Captain Stein, 'I'll call regional HQ and tell them to get us out of here tonight.'

44
Unwanted Visitors

A loud clang of metal bolts echoed around the entrance hall as the huge wooden doors to the clan's headquarters were flung open by Luca Salazar. The heat from outside tainted the cool atmosphere from the stone walls inside and the resident vampires were quick to close the doors once Salazar's squad of five vampires entered the main hall.

Marcus and Roxy emerged from a dark corridor at the opposite end of the hall to meet their visitors. Marcus reluctantly shook hands with Salazar and they nodded to each other, their mutual hatred thinly veiled by an air of civility.

'Good evening, Luca,' said Marcus, 'welcome back to our headquarters.'

It had been a long time since the Deputy Lord Chancellor had visited Marcus Verrico's clan. The Lord Chancellor himself had never visited. He very rarely visited the clans, primarily for security reasons but also to retain his threatening air of mystery.

'I bring best wishes from the Lord Chancellor,' Salazar said, 'He wishes you and your clan all the best in the timely recovery of Doctor Owen.'

Marcus had only met the Lord Chancellor twice in his undead lifetime but he had been in his service for long enough to know the true meaning of his sentiment.

Find the doctor tonight or your clan is finished. Find him or you *are finished.*

'We know where the doctor is being held,' said Marcus, 'We are gathering our forces together and we are poised to launch an attack as soon as I give the word. Please follow me through to our dining hall where we can feast and toast the successful return of Doctor Owen.'

'Thank you,' Salazar said, 'but what makes you think this attack will be more successful than any other? The mortals are well trained and well armed.'

'With respect sir, I must correct you there; that is only partially correct. They are well trained and well armed for a small attack. They believe there are very few of our brothers and sisters in the local area but tonight we will show them our true potential.'

The serious look on Marcus' face told the Deputy Lord Chancellor that he meant business.

'Sounds like you have everything in hand,' Salazar said, trying not to show he was impressed with the Marcus' ambition. He waved a hand towards the dining hall, 'Lead the way, Marcus.'

45
Medical Room

The medical room in Hartley House used to be a banquet hall. Statesmen and the local well-to-do would spend many an evening feasting on suckling pig while dozens of servants buzzed around them.

That had been a long time ago. Now all the furniture was piled in the corner, covered by a thick layer of dust and the priceless paintings that hadn't seen the light of day for years were protected by white sheets. The table that used to seat thirty aristocrats and playboys had been moved to another hall to make room for Doctor Owen's equipment.

Detective Ryder's cold, pale body arrived in the medical room tied to a wheeled stretcher pushed by two very uneasy-looking soldiers. Doctor Owen was waiting, already suited up with a surgical mask over his face.

Everywhere Agent Simpson looked she could see soldiers holding rifles, with their fingers hovering over the triggers. They were nervous about having a bite victim at the outpost. Agent Simpson wondered how many of them had actually seen a live vampire before.

An attack had never happened at this outpost but the soldiers had all heard the horror stories about what can happen. Every outpost that had been infiltrated by a vampire had sustained heavy losses within minutes of the attack. They all knew it could happen to them at any time but now they were face to face with their fears.

The man in front of them could turn into a real life vampire at any moment and rip their bodies to pieces with his bare hands. The more recent recruits were all desperately running through their training in their minds, trying to find the tactics that would help them stay alive if this unfortunate half-dead man in front of them suddenly developed the desire to suck their blood.

In the time she had been a member of the Brotherhood, Agent Simpson was aware of only one time in recent history when an outpost was infiltrated by a vampire. Captain Stein had been in charge of the outpost and had lost many good men: thirty-five soldiers were either killed or reborn and he was the only survivor.

He swore he would never let that happen again. Now he was standing over the bed holding a rifle loaded with silver bullets. One squeeze of the trigger would unload them all into Detective Ryder's body and rid them all of the immediate threat.

'You'll have to back off if I'm going to treat him,' Doctor Owen said as he approached the bed. Captain Stein eyeballed the doctor and reluctantly took a step back.

'Can you help him?' asked Agent Simpson.

'I'm not sure,' said Doctor Owen, 'the wound has stopped bleeding but his heart is still beating. You did good work on his neck to stop the flow. He is unconscious, which is common for a bite victim. How long is it since he was bitten?'

'About twenty minutes', she said, 'How long before he turns?'

'It depends. It can be minutes or hours but he may not even turn. Not every bite victim turns into a vampire. Some get lucky.'

'You have to work on him under the assumption that he could turn at any minute,' said Captain Stein.

'I know, Captain,' Doctor Owen said.

Doctor Owen unzipped a small case containing ten small syringes, each containing a bright yellow liquid. He took one out of the case, wiped down a spot of Detective Ryder's right arm with alcohol and injected the liquid into his vein.

'Now all we can do is wait for him to wake up,' said Doctor Owen.

'Is that it?' asked Agent Simpson, 'Isn't there anything else we can do?'

'Nothing at all. I'd give him a fifty-fifty chance of waking up human. We'll just have to wait and see.' Doctor Owen's words contained no compassion or sympathy. It became clear to Agent Simpson that the doctor had no more feelings for Detective Ryder than he did for the rats in his lab.

Captain Stein turned to the two least nervous-looking soldiers. 'You two stay here.'

'And do what sir?' asked one of them.

Captain Stein rolled his eyes sighed with exasperation. These young recruits were dedicated but some of them were really dumb.

'If he wakes up and shows any sign of being one of *them*,' said Captain Stein, 'shoot him in the head. That's the big round thing at the end of his body. Do you want me to draw you a map?'

'No, sir.'

46
Dreams

I was in a terrible place.

Drifting in and out of consciousness, I was struggling to determine what was real and what wasn't. I wanted to call out for help but couldn't.

The pain in my neck was spreading all over me, like a swarm of insects crawling into every corner of my body and nibbling at my bones and muscles. I was being overcome by something I had never felt before. Every nerve ending was on fire and my limbs felt like they were expanding and contracting over and over again.

My physical body was out of my control. My jaw was cracking and clicking and my front teeth were shifting in their sockets, like they were trying to escape from my mouth.

I heard voices echoing all around me.

Shoot him in the head now!

His heart is still beating.

Isn't there anything else we can do?

Nothing at all.

Then came the visions. Bright colours flashing before me followed by complete darkness. It felt like I was falling down a bottomless pit. More images flashed into my head from the past and present.

Officer Myers, driven by bloodlust, leaping from building to building.

The mutilated body of Danny Johnson lying in the morgue with Doctor Schreiber poking around in his wounds.

Sarah, my beautiful wife, lying battered and bruised on our kitchen floor, her limbs twisted into unnatural shapes.

Standing face to face with my wife's murderer.

Images flashed before my eyes that I didn't recognise.

Running up a flight of stairs with scores of bloodthirsty vampires in pursuit.

Looking down at a severed head in my hands.

How could this happen to me? Twenty-four hours earlier I was just a regular over-worked cop needing a good night's sleep. Now I didn't know if I was going to make it through the night, and if I did, would I be the same person when I woke up?

Am I the same person now?

Will I feel the need to feed on blood every night?

Will I ever wake up?

47

The Most Important Person In The World

Agent Simpson stood outside the door of the medical room, watching the body of Detective Ryder twitch and shake the stretcher he was tightly bound to. The lamps around the room cast oversized shadows on the stone walls, exaggerating his movements and magnifying the pain she felt for him.

He doesn't deserve this, Agent Simpson told herself. His smarts and bravery had helped The Brotherhood find the doctor before he knew what he was getting involved in. He had succeeded with considerably fewer resources than Captain Stein had at his disposal.

She had hidden her intentions from him and was starting to question her methods. If she had told him everything when they first met, would he have been better prepared? If he knew about the war with the vampires from the beginning would he be standing next to her rather than lying on a stretcher, convulsing violently in a fit caused by the experimental treatment Doctor Owen had given him?

But how could I have told him anything? He never would have believed me.

If he didn't pull through, she didn't think she'd be able to forgive herself.

Captain Stein's heavy boots stomped down the hall and stopped next to Agent Simpson.

'Sorry about pulling a gun on you before,' she said, 'I know I broke the rules.'

'You're right,' he replied, 'but you were right about something else. He did help us get to the doctor.'

'How is the doctor?' she asked.

'He's spent the last twenty-four hours in the company of his wife, then vampires, then us. I think he's sleeping now, or trying to at least.'

'Does he know about his wife?'

'Yes, but he's just as worried now that the police have her. She's out in the open now. All it will take to get to her is one infiltrator in the police department. As far as we know, they might already be overrun with bloodsuckers. There's not much we can do about it tonight though.'

'Any news on Doctor Forrest? He wasn't home when we picked up the doctor.'

'No, there's no news on him yet. We're widening the search but if the vampires have him, they'll be keeping him under closer wraps than they did with the doctor.'

'Did you call regional headquarters?'

'Yes. They're sending a couple of helicopters to pick us up. Like you said, we have to assume we're going to be targeted tonight so we'll leave a team behind to take care of them when they arrive.'

Agent Simpson felt slight relief. The helicopters they were sending would undoubtedly be heavily armed and well-manned. They could feel relatively safe on the ride back to regional HQ.

'What about Tom Ryder?' she asked.

'What about him?' Captain Stein seemed taken aback at the suggestion there was any question in the matter. 'We'll patch him up and send him on his way.'

'We can't do that,' said Agent Simpson, raising her voice slightly. One more ignorant comment like that from Captain Stein would tip her over the edge. She had thought she was getting through to him.

'Why not? If he wakes up human he'll be okay.' Captain Stein knew this was an ignorant attitude but he didn't need or want the hassle of taking a potential vampire with them. It was the last straw for Agent Simpson.

'That's not true and you know it!' she argued, 'The treatment is still in the experimental stage. Doctor Owen wants to monitor him and suspects any improvement will only be temporary. Tom Ryder is the best chance for the doctor to move on at an unprecedented rate. He may not look it but he's very excited to have a live specimen to work on.'

Captain Stein's shoulders slumped. 'You're right. We've got to take this guy with us.'

'He's a very important subject. If he has been infected, this will allow us to experiment with the virus like we never have before. The longer he stays human, the more hope we will have for the future.'

A door behind them opened and Doctor Owen emerged. 'She's right, you know. This man is the most important person in the world to us right now. His blood can tell us a hundred times more than we already know and let us take giant leaps in finding a cure.'

Agent Simpson suspected the doctor had been listening to their conversation from behind the door for a while.

'Yes, well you know how I feel about that,' said Captain Stein.

'Yes I do, *Mister* Stein.' He opened the door to the medical room.

'What are you doing?' asked Captain Stein.

'He's been out for exactly three hours. It's time to take another sample.'

As Doctor Owen sat on the edge of the bed and took his fourth blood sample from Detective Ryder, Agent Simpson thought about the exchange of words between the Captain and the doctor.

'You don't think he's going to find a cure, do you?' she asked Captain Stein.

'I think if the doctor works hard enough, he'll find a treatment for the virus.' Stein still didn't seem enthusiastic about this possibility.

'So what do you have a problem with?'

'He shouldn't be looking for a cure. Once someone is reborn they become a member of another species. Pure evil.'

'You know that no scientist has got any proof of that theory but surely the answer can't be killing them all off?'

'Right now it's the only option we have, Agent Simpson.'

48
Infiltration

The regional headquarters of The Brotherhood could be found sitting atop a plateau high in the mountains. It was an effective strategic position: high altitude, maximum hours of sunlight and could only be reached by helicopter unless a potential invader was an expert climber and was prepared to brave the high level of security around the base.

To date, there had not been a single case of vampire infiltration at this base, which housed fifty soldiers and additional medical and administrative staff. The base was well guarded but the outposts suffered occasional losses and from time to time, they had to be evacuated following an attack so there were enough facilities at the regional bases to house at least two hundred tired and hungry soldiers.

The Brotherhood had a very stringent screening process for all new recruits. Or so they thought. The screening process wasn't strict enough.

Private Lambert ran into his private dormitory with five minutes to get ready before he had to join the rest of his squad. It was time for another evacuation: their mission was to extract the squad from the outpost at Hartley House.

In his private room, he took off his training gear and changed into his combat uniform. The soldiers at regional headquarters worked 12-hour shifts and Private Lambert was a member of the night shift, which suited him just fine. He was a vampire.

He wasn't the only vampire at the regional headquarters either. Getting round the checks wasn't as hard as they had thought it might be. Dozens of others had been sacrificed so his brothers and sisters could perfect the art of planting a vampire in The Brotherhood. By the time his turn came, he had a very complex set of instructions to carry out to make the recruitment board believe he was human. In fact, he had been human just a matter of weeks before he became a member of The Brotherhood.

That's because Private Lambert was a consenting recruit. With nothing in his human life other than his drug addiction, he told himself that the only thing to do was to take drastic action. Nothing could be worse than the living hell his life had become so when he was confronted by a vampire looking to feed, he didn't run, cry or try to fight like most members of the human race. No, Private Lambert conceded to his attacker and succumbed to a new life that had to be better than his own.

He had been a vampire for a year and felt his undead life was a significant improvement over his previous life. He was a major player in the ongoing rise of the vampire community. His brothers and sisters were succeeding in infiltrating every part of human life, even the war effort against them.

Most of the world governments had members from the vampire community; even some of the human world leaders supported their cause. The emergency services were a primary target for infiltration. This strategy allowed the vampire brothers and sisters to get away with just about anything. No matter what crime against humanity they were arrested and detained for, the vampires almost always managed to evade justice or get off on a technicality.

Private Lambert pulled the drawer all the way out of his desk and removed a mobile phone that was taped to the back. He dialled the number for his true regional headquarters and spoke to Roxy, his true leader.

Even though he had good news, he was still worried about talking to Roxy. Her reputation preceded her. Vampires that hadn't even met Roxy knew the stories about her. She was merciless and wouldn't think twice about dispatching her brothers and sisters if ordered to do so.

'Yes, Private Lambert. What information do you have?' she demanded. No pleasantries, no nonsense.

'Our squad will be leaving in the next few minutes,' he said, 'and will arrive at Hartley House in approximately one hour. Our mission is to extract the squad and their visitors, including Doctor Owen.'

There was a silence on the line as Roxy formulated her plan. 'We will launch the attack once you arrive. That will maximise the impact on their numbers. Soften them up for our arrival.'

Private Lambert suspected that would be her plan. She wanted to take out as many humans as possible, but what should they do with them: kill them or turn them into vampires? He put the question to her.

'We will turn them,' she said immediately, 'but you must make sure their attacking potential is reduced as much as possible.'

'Understood. You can count on me.' Private Lambert hoped it didn't sound like he was brown-nosing. He didn't get any indication of Roxy's opinion of him though; she hung up before he could say any more.

For our *arrival*, he thought. Roxy was leading the attack, which meant this was a very important mission. He could hardly wait.

Humans are naïve and stupid: they believe the vampires' numbers are small. How wrong they are.

49
Fine Wine

The Deputy Lord Chancellor waved his empty glass in the air and a servant of the clan rushed over with a jug to fill it up. The thick, dark red liquid poured into his glass. Luca Salazar lifted the glass to his nose and took a deep breath. He swirled the wine around then took a sip.

'How do you find the wine?' Marcus asked. He was sitting at the opposite end of a long table in the stone walled dining hall. Flaming torches lit the hall and the crackling logs in the huge roaring fireplace kept both diners warm.

Luca Salazar licked his lips in appreciation. 'Very good,' he said. Marcus believed him as well. Salazar had complained about most of the meal but he knew he would like the dessert wine. All vampires did.

'Where did you get it? I don't recognise the taste.'

'We make it ourselves,' Marcus said.

'Really? I didn't realise you had a farm.'

'Yes, I've been producing wine for many centuries. I learned from the best. The farm is a long way out of the city, hidden away from the humans. Only a few of us know where it is.'

'I'm not surprised. If I could make wine of this quality, I'd keep my methods secret as well. I would increase the production if I were you. I will recommend it to the Lord Chancellor and he may want to place an order.'

Marcus rolled his eyes but Salazar didn't notice this show of disdain from a subordinate. *It was just like a senior vampire to sit up there on his high horse, looking down on those of us doing the real work. He has no idea what goes into making a wine of this quality.*

Making a wine as good as the vintage that Salazar was sampling took hard work and patience. There was only one harvest per year. The specimens took twenty years to ripen, fed daily on the best foodstuffs and only the best were picked to make it into the premium wine.

The specimens are taken to the kitchen, slaughtered and their blood is drained into the bottling machine. The leftover human skins and muscles are then put to good use. The steaks they had both eaten had come from human bodies. While Marcus' steak had come from the rump of a premium body, Salazar's had come from a rejected body.

He always complains about the food so why waste a good meal on him?

'The next specimens will be harvested soon,' Marcus said, 'I personally oversee the harvest myself every year and I will ensure a case of the finest wine is produced for the Lord Chancellor.'

Salazar nodded, 'Very good idea. He will appreciate that.'

Servants opened the doors to the dining hall and Roxy entered. 'Sir, may I have a word?' she asked Marcus.

'Of course. What is it, Roxy?'

'I have just had confirmation of Doctor Owen's location. The Brotherhood are evacuating their outpost and returning to their regional headquarters. We will strike when the extraction team arrives at the outpost.'

Salazar butted in. 'Is that wise?'

'Excuse me?' asked Roxy. The look on her face showed she had as little respect for the Deputy Lord Chancellor as Marcus did.

'If you are going to attack The Brotherhood, surely it would be a better idea to attack when their numbers are fewer.'

'That may seem like the easy option but this is not the usual kind of mission. One of our brothers is a member of the extraction team. Our plan is to sabotage the infrastructure and reduce their capability. A large unit in a state of panic is a much easier target than a small well-prepared unit.'

Salazar didn't answer. *That shut him up*, Roxy thought.

'Also,' she continued unopposed, 'we are using this attack as an opportunity to demonstrate our military capability. There has not been an attack of this size in a very long time. We have previously only operated in groups of ten or fewer.'

'How many of our brothers and sisters will be joining this attack?' Salazar asked.

'One hundred,' she said.

Salazar's eyes widened and apart from the noise of the burning fire, there were a few seconds of silence in the dining hall. He turned to address Marcus. 'I would wish her good luck but I don't think she's going to need it. Her squad are sure to have a greater feast than we have enjoyed this evening.'

Marcus raised his glass and nodded in agreement.

50
The Rising Begins

Deep within the subterranean lair of the vampires where no human had ever ventured, no human would dare to venture if they knew what would be down there waiting for them.

In a gigantic dark cavern, one hundred well-trained vampires were honing their skills. Scores of the creatures clung to the walls then flew in formation across the vast expanse, repeating their movements over and over again until they flew as one airborne killing machine.

The remaining vampires lined the cavern floor, sparring with their steel swords, moving in gravity-defying leaps that the poor kids who passed themselves off as soldiers of The Brotherhood would find both terrifying and amazing seconds before they were sliced to pieces.

Roxy carefully opened the door to the training hall and stepped inside unnoticed. She stood in the shadows, admiring the results of her work as a leader. Her brothers and sisters had gone through years of punishing training to reach these heights of physical and tactical perfection. They moved as one, their swords an extension of their arms and they shared one desire, just like all vampires.

To feed. At the expense of all other life.

Roxy stepped out of the darkness and made her way to the centre of the cavern. Those who noticed her tall imposing figure slink past stopped what they were doing and stood to attention.

Slowly but surely, the silent deference spread through the hall like a wave and all one hundred vampires made their way to the middle of the floor, either marching or swooping down from the walls, eager to hear what their leader had to say.

'Tonight is a very important night,' she began, knowing there was no chance of this speech being interrupted. 'Tonight is the night you have been training for all of your life. Tonight is the night we will show the world the true power of our species. We will not stay in the darkness forever. We will rise up and take our rightful place as the dominant force in this world.

'I'm not going to lie to you,' she continued, 'not all of you will make it back. But you can be sure that you are serving a higher purpose and very shortly a blow will be struck that will echo around the world. Alive or dead, each and every one of you will have your place in history. In years to come our people will look back on this day and know that it was the day when it all began. Now let's get out there and show them what we can do. Hit them. Hit them hard.'

The premature roar of victory echoed throughout the hall.

51
Awake

A sharp pain in my arm awoke me from my nightmare.

I opened my eyes to find a man in a white coat and a mask sticking a needle into me. His brown eyes widened and he took a step back. I tried to sit up but couldn't move: I was strapped to my bed very tightly.

'Hello Detective Ryder, I'm Doctor Owen,' the man in white said, and started to loosen my straps. I heard the click of a gun somewhere in the room. 'What do you think you're doing?' someone asked.

'He's perfectly fine,' Doctor Owen said as he unbuckled my straps. Very slowly, I sat up and hung my legs over the side of the bed.

I felt like I had the worst hangover of my life. I could feel all the tell-tale sensations running through my body, only more intense.

'How do you feel?' the doctor asked.

'Light headed. Thirsty. Very hungry. It feels like I've got pins and needles all over my body. And the worst headache I've ever had,' I said, cupping my forehead with both hands.

'Interesting,' he said as he leaned over me and shone a light in my eyes. A sharp bolt of pain hit me like a punch to the head.

'Damn it! What did you do that for?' I shouted.

'Sorry,' he said and handed me two paracetamol tablets. I grabbed the bottle out of his other hand and knocked back a mouthful. I shuddered as the sharp chalky taste went down my throat. *They can make pills that can take away headaches but why can't they make them taste better?*

He then opened my mouth and examined my teeth. He turned to talk to someone behind him. 'I think the treatment has worked. He is still human for now.'

That's when I remembered what had happened. I had been bitten by a vampire on the bonnet of my car. A vampire that used to be one of my only friends in the world.

I looked at the odd surroundings. I seemed to be in some kind of fancy room that looked like it belonged in a stately home or a palace; however the appliances and the doctor's clothing would have been more appropriate in an operating theatre. A muted television in the corner showed a reporter at the site of the gunship attack.

'How long will he stay like this?' I realised who that voice belonged to. It was Captain Stein. *I must be in the presence of The Brotherhood.*

'At least twelve hours,' said the doctor, 'maybe twenty-four.'

'Okay, get him up. We're not taking any chances though,' said Captain Stein. Two soldiers appeared and pointed their rifles in my face.

'What's going on? What are they doing?' I asked.

'We'll have plenty of time to talk about this. Don't worry. It's important you tell me how you're feeling,' the doctor said.

'Very thirsty, can I have some water?' I asked.

The doctor gave me a litre bottle. I swallowed the whole lot quickly in big gulps and asked for more. I then registered that my body was very clammy and the bed sheets I had been lying on were soaked through.

'What the hell happened to me?' I asked.

'Your temperature went sky high,' said Doctor Owen, 'your body has been working overtime to fight the virus.' My hand immediately went to my neck and I felt a massive bandage covering the wound.

'You also lost about two pints of blood.' As I took more big gulps from another bottle of water, more questions occurred to me about my condition.

'So what's the deal, Doc? Am I a vampire?'

'It's too early to say,' he said, 'The treatment I've been working on seems to have kept the virus at bay for now but you and I are going to be spending a lot of time together. I need to take samples from you on the hour every hour so we can see how the virus develops. From that data, we can work towards a cure.'

Data? Is that what I've become? 'Hey, I'm not your lab rat, Doc.'

'No, Detective Ryder, you are so much more than that. The chemical reactions currently taking place in your body may hold the key to eradicating vampires from existence. We have to work together for the good of mankind.'

He certainly did his best to make lying in bed getting stuck with needles sound like a noble cause. Needless to say, that wasn't how I'd pictured my future.

'Wait a minute, I'm a cop. This is my case and I've already worked out that the vampires blew up your lab. It's going to be difficult to write that up in my report but I'll manage. Case closed.' I got up and started to wobble towards the door.

'Twenty-four hours,' the doctor announced, rather cryptically.

I stopped and turned round to look at him. 'What happens in twenty-four hours?'

'That's how long you have left until you turn,' he said.

'You mean the stuff you gave me runs out?'

'I believe it will, and twenty-four hours is almost certainly an optimistic estimate. It may be twelve hours, which means you need to be treated at least once a day. You can't go back to your job. You're too important to us and you have no choice.'

I didn't want to agree with him but he was right. I couldn't just close the case and walk away. My discoveries today had changed my life. I couldn't just leave this war with the vampires and I definitely didn't want to become one of *them.*

If I choose to leave, will I end up with silver bullets in my back like Officer Myers as soon as I walk through the door?

'We need you, Detective,' he continued, 'you're the best chance we've ever had.'

Do I really have a choice?

'Okay,' I said reluctantly, 'what do we need to do?'

52
Plans

Doctor Owen and I were left alone in the medical room to talk about his plans for me.

His plans for me.

Last time I had checked, I was a cop with a job that ran my life but I knew that any day I could just quit, go home and never set foot in a police station again.

Now I had to come to terms with the fact that I was going to be a guinea pig for different types of experimental medical treatment. I was going to be the right hand man to the scientist who would produce a vaccine that would rid the world of vampires forever. I can't say I wasn't a little excited about the whole thing. At this moment in time I was the most important human being in the world. The key to unlocking the secret of the vampires.

'Don't go getting delusions of grandeur,' said Doctor Owen jovially with a knowing smile on his face, immediately bursting my balloon, 'there have been people like you before. They all got a bit carried away with their place in the world and thought they were invincible. They took risks they shouldn't have and we were back to square one.

'The top priority in your life is to keep both of us alive. If you die then we're back to square one again, and if I die, you die.'

Now who's getting delusions of grandeur?

'You may think of me as arrogant but they are the facts, Detective. It's an unfortunate situation that you find yourself in but we must make the most of it. Okay?'

I nodded in agreement and that was it, my new life had begun. First thing in the morning I would call into work and quit. Just like that. One day a cop, the next day a scientific sample. My thoughts immediately turned to how I would pay the bills from now on.

'You don't need to worry about the bare necessities, The Brotherhood will take care of everything for you,' he said, as if he was reading my mind. It seemed to me that he had answered all of these questions a thousand times before and knew exactly what I was going to ask before I opened my mouth.

It made me uneasy. *How many guinea pigs have there been before and why aren't they here any more?*

The doctor continued. 'They'll give you a bed and three meals a day. If you rent your home, call your landlord and cancel the payments. If you own your home, put it up for sale.'

'Okay Doc, what do you need from me?'

'I need to take blood samples from you on the hour every hour until further notice. That means right through the night and all day tomorrow. During this time we have to gather as many samples as we can. It's going to be hard work.'

'Don't worry, I'm used to sacrificing sleep for work.' I tried my best to sound committed to the cause. If we were going to work together for the rest of my life, we'd better start off in the right way.

'Good,' he said and smiled sympathetically. The look on his face told me he was thinking he wouldn't trade places with me for all the tea in China.

Time to ask the hard questions. 'What's going to happen to me? How will I know if I'm turning into a vampire?'

'That's a good question. We've never been able to identify all of the symptoms because the previous subjects have turned too quickly to allow them to tell us what's happening to them. At the very least I hope the treatment can delay or slow down the virus so we can have time to see what it does to your body.'

'That's not very comforting, Doc.'

'I'm not here to hold your hand and tell you everything's going to be okay, Detective. I'm here to tell you the way it is. No bullshit.' He was right, but it didn't make the situation any better.

I looked at the television in the corner again, which was still showing clips of the damage inflicted on the tactical aid unit by my new hosts. I asked the doctor to turn up the volume so I could hear the reporter.

'We've just had confirmation from the hospital,' the female reporter began ominously, 'that the only member of the tactical aid unit to survive this afternoon's attack has just passed away. Other than varying eye witness accounts, the only law enforcer to see today's events first-hand was Detective Tom Ryder, who is unavailable for comment.'

That's an understatement, I thought.

'However, we managed to speak to Captain Nash of the police department early today.'

Among the scrolling headlines and weather report icons, Captain Nash appeared, standing on the front steps of police headquarters. 'The attack this afternoon was a targeted attempt to remove the capabilities of the police, who were just about to arrest the perpetrators.'

A number of reporters all asked if Nash knew who the attackers were. His reply was only 'I'm sorry, I can't comment on that.'

The news broadcast then returned to the reporter. 'If the police know anything, they are keeping their cards very close to their chest. It seems to me that an investigation is underway and the police have their suspicions of who committed this terrible attack. After the lives lost and the damage caused on the freeway today, you have to ask yourself a question. Do the police have the firepower to counter another attack like this?'

'Nash knows a hell of a lot more than that,' I said, 'why didn't they mention the missing doctors?'

'You have a lot to learn,' said Doctor Owen, 'Even though you've only just found out the truth, there are already many out there that know everything and work for The Brotherhood.'

'What? You're saying that my boss knows about all this?'

'It's likely he knows something. You can never know for sure. Only a few select people have access to the records.'

'The records?'

'The Brotherhood maintain a list of allies and their positions within society. The police, government, everywhere. This is a tactic also employed by the vampires though, so when you meet someone, you can never really tell which side they're on or if they're just a regular Joe.'

'But what about the press? Not every journalist can be on your side.'

'That's right. Sometimes reports get through in the early editions or if the editor hasn't spoken to the reporter on TV before they go on air. Those mistakes are few and far between and the network always manages to change its tune before anyone notices.'

There was no time to let this sink in before Captain Stein burst into the medical room. 'Pack all that crap away;' he bellowed, 'we're pulling out in five minutes.' He left as quickly as he had arrived, slamming the door behind him.

53

The Only Difference

The night air was still and cool, easing the heat within the soldiers' uniforms as they carried out their tasks before the arrival of the extraction team. Captain Stein stood on the front steps, barking orders at everyone. Most of the soldiers were running around, gathering together as much of the outpost's equipment as they could.

Far away on the horizon, two gunships were just visible, approaching from the mountains to collect the inhabitants of the outpost and take them to the regional headquarters where they would be better protected. Captain Stein and his contacts at the regional headquarters all suspected there would be an attack. The question was: could they get out of there in time?

Three tall wooden structures stood in grassy clearings. They were lookout towers, each holding a supply of ammunition and sun block, which every soldier hoped would be enough to deal with any attack.

The remaining soldiers were climbing ladders into the wooden towers with their rifles and silver-plated swords strapped to their backs. When each soldier reached the top, they pulled the cord above them to illuminate the protective ultraviolet lamps and adorned themselves with standard-issue wraparound sunglasses.

The fact of the matter was that with the exception of Captain Stein, no one else at Hartley House had participated in a major battle. A lot of them had never even seen a real vampire.

Private Brown stood at the top of his tower and checked that his rifle was loaded. Then he picked up a bottle of sunscreen, squirted a big dollop into his hands and rubbed it into every exposed area on his body. He then checked his rifle again.

Don't worry, he told himself, *this is an exercise just like any other. I've watched over dozens of extractions and they've all gone perfectly smoothly. There's no reason why this won't go according to plan.*

Private Brown cast his eyes around the grounds and saw the one thing that made this exercise different. Doctor Owen appeared on the front steps of Hartley House.

54
Easy Shift

Private Moore was sitting under a tree in the darkness, enjoying the easy shift. Every four weeks, the soldiers had to take the journey out to one of the dugouts hidden in the fields on the one-mile radius around Hartley House. Their job was to keep a watchful eye on the skies for approaching bloodsuckers but since there hadn't been any vampire activity for a long time, everyone in the squad looked forward to the lookout shift as an opportunity to chill out and get some extra shut-eye.

The soldiers on the easy shift all kept in touch with each other on a different radio channel that wasn't being monitored by their colleagues at Hartley House and took it in turns to sleep. Private Moore looked at his watch.

Time to catch some zees.

He picked up his radio and changed the channel. 'Time's up, dude. It's my turn now,' he said, expecting his squad mate Private Norris to answer him, but there was no reply.

'Hey, are you there? Wake up you lazy son of a bitch.'

Again, all he heard was interference on the radio.

'Is anyone else out there? Anyone seen Pete tonight?'

There was no answer again for a few seconds until he heard the friendly voice of Private Wilson. 'Hey, it's Mike here. I haven't seen him or heard from him. Thinking about it, I haven't heard from anyone for a while.'

'Come on guys,' Moore said into the radio, 'no messing around tonight. Who's out there?'

After another moment of radio static, Private Wilson answered again. 'Looks like it's just me and you. I wonder what's going on. Oh shit, wait a minute.'

'What's going on, Mike?'

'Look up. To the east.'

Private Moore grabbed his rifle and got to his feet. He looked to the east but couldn't see anything out of the ordinary. Just a big black cloud.

Just a big black cloud that's moving towards me.

'What the hell's going on, Mike?' Private Moore shouted into the radio and got a one word answer that made his heart sink.

'Incoming!'

He heard the sound of gunfire in the distance and ran into the middle of his field to make a stand against the dark cloud coming his way. Realising he had left his radio under the tree, Moore checked his rifle was loaded and flicked the safety catch, hoping to keep his worst nightmare at bay long enough to get back to warn everyone at Hartley House.

Who am I kidding? I'm a dead man, he thought.

He was right.

55
Agent Simpson

Jane Simpson sat on a wooden bench in the grounds of Hartley House. It had been a hard day and she needed to take a few minutes to gather her thoughts together before they would be on the move again.

Poor Detective Ryder. Poor Tom.

He had no idea what lay ahead for him. Doctor Owen had sat him down in the medical room and was telling him how he was the future saviour of humanity but probably not going into the details of what would be expected of him when they all arrived at regional headquarters. Captain Stein was tough but she knew Commander North would be ten times worse.

He's already expecting results. And he wants them sooner than is physically possible

It was a true shame. That morning, he'd just been another homicide detective, now he was kissing goodbye to his life in the name of science.

If only we'd met under other circumstances. Rough around the edges of course, but there's something there.

She had enjoyed their short time working together. Their brief partnership had been very successful. He knew what he was doing and they got results. The Brotherhood now had the doctor but she couldn't help thinking that if she'd been straight with Detective Ryder from the beginning, if she'd only told him that she was a member of The Brotherhood, he wouldn't be looking at a life as Doctor Owen's pin cushion.

Then there was Doctor Owen himself. Snatched from a motel as he made his half-assed escape.

How did the vampires know about his work and where he was staying? Who was he really running from?

The vampire community must have found out that he had reached a breakthrough stage in the secondary treatment at the same time

The Brotherhood had found out, maybe even before. Sure, there were spies and double agents on both sides but only a select few knew the details of the scientific research.

Who really wants Doctor Owen to stop his work on the secondary treatment?

Jane Simpson shook her head, trying to rid the logical answer to that question from her mind. The very idea was preposterous and she refused to consider it.

Somehow the vampires had found out that a cure for their blood disorder was within reach and were taking the measures necessary to ensure their way of life could survive. If The Brotherhood could recover Doctor Forrest, they would have control of all the available intellectual capital and could move the research forward securely.

Then something else occurred to her and she kicked herself that she hadn't thought of it before. Something that no one had mentioned since the attack on Mantek and she was certain that Brotherhood weren't prepared for a large-scale attack.

If the vampires knew their way of life was in danger, they would surely do everything they could to protect themselves. If they're willing to take drastic action to protect their numbers, how many of them are there?

56
Live Each Day As If It Were Your Last

The doctor and I stepped outside Hartley House to see many soldiers running around, stacking equipment into piles on the drive. Captain Stein was coordinating the efforts, shouting at anyone and everyone.

His coercive approach appeared to work. He gave the nod to approve the completion of the soldiers' tasks then sent them off to stand guard over the patch of grass where the helicopters were expected to land.

I spotted three wooden towers, each housing two soldiers armed with rifles and swords. The sunscreen painted on their faces was illuminated by the ultraviolet lamps hanging above them.

'How safe is it up there?' I asked the doctor, 'If any vampires attacked, wouldn't they just chop the towers down?'

'The vampires attack in small numbers,' he said, 'they're fairly easy to pick off from up there and the UV light provides enough protection.'

'Why do they attack in small numbers?'

'All evidence points towards a small population. We suspect their numbers are low. There hasn't been a large scale attack on a human population for over fifty years.'

I was still worried about the soldiers in the tower and it must have shown on my face.

'Don't worry,' said Doctor Owen, 'we'll be out of here in no time. Look, here they come.'

In the distance I could see two helicopters flying towards us, the same kind of gunships that had picked up Captain Stein from the shootout earlier that day.

I felt a hand on my shoulder and heard a friendly voice in my ear. 'How are you feeling, Detective?' I spun round and was faced with Agent Simpson. She was definitely a sight for sore eyes.

'Not too bad, considering I might be one of the Lost Boys.' Not the funniest line to emerge from my lips but it got a wry smile at least.

'You've been through a lot today,' she said, 'once we get you back to regional headquarters, you'll be able to get some rest. The compound is heavily guarded and very secure. You can feel safe there.'

'You mean you don't feel safe with those guys up there in the wooden sun beds?' I asked.

'They've fought off plenty of attacks before. Don't worry, Detective,' she said. I suspected she was lying about the level of experience these soldiers had, but she was only trying to ease my worries.

'That's what he said,' I replied, thumbing in the direction of Doctor Owen, 'And please, call me Tom. I'm not a detective any more, remember?'

'So you've decided to stay?' she asked, with a sparkle in her eye.

'I don't have much choice, do I Jane?'

'You've always got a choice,' she said, 'they didn't all decide to stay.'

'Who's *they*?' I asked, knowing exactly who she was talking about.

'The guinea pigs before you. There have been quite a few but not all of them decided to stay.'

'What happened to them?'

'We're not sure but it's safe to assume they either died or joined the vampire clan.'

'And what about the ones that stayed? I take it they all made a remarkable recovery and are now living happy and fulfilling lives?' I asked in a tone both hopeful and sarcastic.

Agent Simpson smiled. 'As far as you know, Tom, yes they did.'

Her positive attitude made me think about the motivational speakers I've listened to down the years at police functions. Every story had the same moral: live each day as if it was your last. I had no option but to take that advice from now on.

If Doctor Owen was going to find a cure, we would need these soldiers and more to hold off all the vampires in the world for as long as his work would take. Having seen the vampires in action already, I hoped Captain Stein had enough new recruits waiting to sign up. If the vampires decided to attack, there would surely be a high turnover of recruits.

I watched the helicopters moving towards us, in anticipation of the secure environment we would soon find ourselves in. Then I noticed a bright flash from one of the helicopters.

Captain Stein ran out of Hartley House onto the front steps, shouting into a radio. 'How many of them?'

'Just one,' was the frantic reply.

'What's the damage?' he shouted.

'He set off a grenade. They're going down, Captain.'

'What happened to him?'

The only reply was machine gun fire, which matched more bright flashes from the helicopter in the distance. Agent Simpson grabbed my arm and dragged me back inside Hartley House as one of the approaching helicopters slowly fell out of the sky.

57
Alpha One Down

Helicopter Alpha One plunged out of the sky as if in slow motion, carrying a squad of doomed soldiers towards an inevitable fiery grave. As they fell, they were doing all they could to kill Private Lambert.

He had followed his orders with dedication and precision. Once Hartley House appeared in the distance, he had pulled the pin out of a hand grenade and thrown it into the cockpit. When it exploded, the fate of the squad was sealed. Private Lambert then clicked the safety catch off his rifle and began to unload it on his squad mates, who followed suit in a blind panic.

Silver bullets rattled around the helicopter, all of the soldiers desperately trying to stop Private Lambert escaping but receiving the gunshots themselves. Seconds before impact, Private Lambert made a leap for freedom and found himself outside the helicopter.

Then he felt a pain in his left foot. He looked at his leg to see his foot dissolve into dust and crumble away. His boot fell from his body towards the ground. One of the stray bullets had hit him. His body would completely disappear in a matter of seconds. There wasn't much time to complete his mission.

He had already taken out one helicopter and had to try his best to slow down the second. If he kept it as far away as possible from Hartley House, the squad on the ground would spread out and be easier to pick off one by one by his brothers and sisters who weren't far away. He could feel the mass of his body getting lighter as the ash blew away below him.

There's not much time.

He looked down and saw a small swarm of soldiers spreading out across the grounds. They were firing their guns in his direction but the bullets were easy to dodge at this distance.

Private Lambert fired his rifle at helicopter Alpha Two, taunting all the soldiers that were trying in vain to kill him. When the forces on the ground started to scatter and fire their weapons in different directions, he knew his plan had worked. The forces at Hartley House were no longer working as a single cohesive unit.

Easy pickings.

A huge cloud of his brothers and sisters was descending on the small band of soldiers below. A hundred vampires, all with an uncontrollable bloodlust and a desire to demonstrate the true might of the species at the top of the food chain.

He almost felt sorry for the soldiers of The Brotherhood. From now on, things will only get worse for them and their kind. A bullet hit him square chest but didn't feel any pain in his body or his mind. He knew he could leave his undead life the way he had always wanted: as a martyr to the cause.

58
Not A Chance

Captain Stein couldn't believe his eyes. All the intelligence available to The Brotherhood had suggested that the vampire community was relatively small, maybe only one hundred of them in the city but now there was at least that number attacking their outpost, maybe more. That intelligence had taken a lot of time and money to gather together and it was useless.

How many other fallacies do we believe without question?

He had only twenty or so men to mount a defence and keep the doctor alive.

We haven't got a chance.

At least there were no surprises in the vampires' armoury. They all carried guns but rarely used them. Their weapon of choice was a sword. When a vampire attacks, it rarely wants to kill you. Their motivation is survival: to feed and increase their numbers. Captain Stein was struggling to believe they had increased their numbers to such an unprecedented level.

If the vampires were to use their guns, all they would achieve would be a pile of useless dead bodies. By slicing everyone up with swords, they could immobilise the targets, feed on the bodies and turn them into vampires. Their favourite tactic was to chop your arms and legs off then come back later to finish you off. Once your rebirth is complete, you grow the missing limbs back anyway.

The vampire army was moving in waves. They had split up into five groups, each flying in a line of ten pairs. The vampires in front led their line in a long, graceful arc high in the air then down on top of the unfortunate soldiers below, slicing and chopping their prey with their long swords. Captain Stein watched in a state of amazed terror. It was an awe-inspiring sight: beautiful yet terrifying.

Four soldiers were positioned on the steps in front of Hartley House, taking shots at the closest vampires. The attack on the helicopters had spread most of the other soldiers out across the grounds, and they were being picked off one by one with embarrassing ease.

The men in the wooden towers were having more luck. Protected by ultraviolet light, they were able to shoot down many of the vampires as they flew past in waves. Stein knew it was only a matter of time until the vampires pulled the towers down. By that time, both he and the doctor had to be on the remaining helicopter, on their way to safety.

When he was satisfied that the men were in the best positions to keep their attackers at bay until the remaining gunship arrived, he lifted his rifle and started to fire silver bullets at the waves of vampires sweeping down on the men in the field. He hit one and it turned to ash before the body hit the ground. Then he hit another, and another, but they just kept coming.

A team of vampires swooped down towards the front steps. Some of them were caught in the crossfire and their burning bodies rained ash down on the soldiers. Two vampires touched down among the soldiers and drew their swords. In a flash, they had disposed of everyone in their path.

Captain Stein turned his rifle on one of the vampires but when he pulled the trigger, the only sound he heard was a disappointingly familiar click.

Damn, out of ammo.

He threw the rifle to the ground and drew his sword just as the vampire drew its sword and swung it towards his head. Their swords met with a clang and Stein immediately knew this wasn't one of the strongest vampires he'd met. After two more parries, he found an opening and jammed his silver-plated sword into his adversary's forehead.

The body was still burning as he moved across the steps to take on another vampire, who was now feasting on one of his men. The vampire noticed him approaching and looked up with blood dripping from his chin. It had no time to attack before Stein sliced its head off, bringing down the sword down in the same move onto the soldier's neck. He took a step back and watched both heads roll down the steps.

Stein wished he didn't have to kill his own men but he had no choice. It was either death or spend the rest of eternity as one of *them.*

He heard the thud of boots hitting the ground behind him and turned around to see a tall, female vampire dressed in black. He knew exactly who this was. They had met once before but had never fought each other.

With a cold, determined look on her face, Roxy stared Stein in the eye and drew her steel sword.

59
Holding Them Off

Private Brown frantically reloaded his rifle for the third time, fumbling with the clip in a desperate rush to continue shooting the demons that were trying to kill him and the rest of his squad.

From his wooden tower, he had a good view of the action below and had already ended the undead lives of at least ten vampires so far, but they just kept coming. He was amazed by the ferocity of this attack and the size of the clan. He had never heard of an attack of this size.

The soldiers on the ground were being slaughtered and it wouldn't be long until the attack turned to the towers. The vampires attacked in waves, swooping down in long groups, cutting the soldiers to pieces. The men on the ground were desperately shooting at their attackers. Some vampires were taken down but still the attacks came. There were just too many of them for a small squad like this to deal with.

The supplies of ammunition in the tower were beginning to dwindle. At this rate they would run out within a matter of minutes.

Brown's squad mate Private Hays was taking pot shots at the band of vampires approaching their tower. Brown's rifle made a click to tell him it was reloaded and ready for action and he joined in the attack.

Looking over the edge of the steel-reinforced side of the tower, he counted at least fifteen vampires approaching them. Brown hit one and its body dissolved into ash. The remaining vampires spread out to make targeting for the soldiers in the tower more difficult.

'Shit!' cursed Private Brown, 'we haven't got long now.' He wiped the sweat from his forehead, only to wipe the sunscreen off his face, which made the heat from the ultraviolet lamps even more unbearable.

'The chopper's almost here,' said Private Hays, 'we've just got to keep them away from the house for a few more minutes.'

'They're flanking us,' said Brown as the group spread out even further and began to surround the tower. He leaned over the side but before he could take a shot, the vampires all drew their guns and began shooting at the top of the tower. Brown and Hays hit the deck.

'What are they doing?' shouted Hays over the sound of gunshots, 'I've never seen them using their guns before.'

I've never seen them before at all, Brown thought to himself.

They both looked up as they heard the ultraviolet lamp smash above them. Fear gripped the soldiers as the gunshots ceased and glass rained down as silent darkness descended on the tower.

Hays and Brown both jumped to their feet and drew their swords just in time to take the heads off two vampires who had leapt to the top of the tower. The ash from their bodies blew away in the wind and another two vampires appeared to replace them. Then another two. And another two. They all drew their swords.

Resigned to their fate, Hays and Brown stood in the middle of the tower, back to back, swinging their swords at the approaching bloodsuckers. They stood their ground with honour but it was only a matter of time before Brown presented an opening and felt a cold sharp blade penetrate his side.

Brown looked down and saw the red blade emerge from his chest. He sank to his knees and with his last ounce of strength, swung his sword through the legs of two of his attackers.

As he fell flat on his face and succumbed to unconsciousness, the last sounds he heard were the agonised screams of Private Hays.

60
One On One

Captain Stein took a deep breath and gripped his silver-plated sword with both hands. He completely focused his mind and body on the next few seconds. He blocked out his peripheral vision and stared directly at Roxy. No other vampires would dare attack him while he was fighting with their leader. She didn't tolerate interference and wouldn't hesitate to cut down her brothers and sisters if they got in the way of a fair fight.

With swords raised, Roxy and Captain Stein took a small step towards each other. They looked into each other's eyes for a few seconds, then Roxy swung her sword at Stein's body. He parried the blow but didn't have time to swing at her before she came at him again.

It was like sparring practice with Private Brown again, only this time Captain Stein was on the back foot. He had fought vampires enough times to know he shouldn't underestimate their strength. Female vampires were notoriously brutal but he was still surprised how much he was struggling. She was putting incredible power behind her blows. Stein was doing all he could just to get his sword between himself and Roxy's.

Just when Stein thought he was done for, he got a chance. Roxy swung her sword and he blocked the blow with more force than he'd been able to muster until now. The sword flew out of her hands and clattered down the steps.

He had his opening. A flash of shock swept across Roxy's face as Stein swung his sword at her with all his might. She just managed to dive out of the way and Stein's blade narrowly missed her torso. She hit the ground and rolled away from the steps, then jumped to her feet and drew her silver sword in time to block Stein's second attack.

Stein had failed to capitalise on the opening and Roxy was on top again, now fighting with more force and edging him backwards, towards the steps. One blow was too hard for him and he lost his footing. He landed on the steps on his side and painfully rolled down to the bottom, his head and joints banging into the edges of the steps.

He shook off the pain in his head and looked around him. Roxy's steel sword was just within reach. Still with his silver sword in his right hand, he picked it up in his left and spun round in time to use it to block Roxy's attack. As she moved forward again, he saw another opening and knew he had to take it. Her legs were exposed so he swung his silver sword with his right hand, slicing them open above the ankles.

Roxy fell backwards onto the steps and looked down at her legs. Ash was already pouring from the wounds. She turned over onto her front and quickly crawled up the steps towards the piles of ash and weapons where the vampires had attacked Captain Stein, looking for a steel sword. Even as her body was dissolving, she was cool and focused under pressure.

She found what she was looking for next to a decapitated soldier's body and grabbed it with both hands. She turned over and raised just it in time to parry a blow from Captain Stein. Before Stein could swing at her again, she leapt into the air and quickly used the sword to chop what was left of her legs off above the spreading wounds.

Stein drew his gun and fired shots at Roxy, but failed to hit her as she flew into the darkness above him. He resigned himself to having missed his opportunity to take out a senior vampire but was happy to have made it through the fight alive. He quickly looked around to assess the immediate danger to him and his men.

He saw one of the wooden towers topple over. The soldiers in the remaining two were unloading their rifles on the vampires crawling up towards them. So much for the ultraviolet lamps: they didn't appear to be doing anything to keep the vampires away from the soldiers in the towers. They had no chance of survival. All they could do was try to send as many of these devils back to hell as they could.

The soldiers in the field were all dead and a large crowd of vampires was advancing on Hartley House. The troops in the remaining helicopter were fending off a swarm of vampires as it made its way towards the house, but their ammunition would only last so long. The helicopter would reach the house in a matter of seconds.

'Alpha Two, this is Captain Stein. Head for the roof,' he shouted into his radio, 'we'll be there in sixty seconds.'

He looked around for the doctor and the detective.

Where the hell are they?

61
Getting Out

Agent Simpson and I followed the doctor as he ran down the long empty halls of Hartley House to the medical room. He picked up some holdalls and threw them at us.

'Fill them up with as much as you can,' he shouted, 'the helicopter will be here in a matter of seconds.'

I threw my arm around a desk full of equipment and papers and scooped it all into my bag. I zipped it up and threw it over my back. Doctor Owen carefully and swiftly closed his cases of test tubes and syringes and placed them into a sturdy metal box.

From deep inside Hartley House, I could still hear the carnage outside. I hoped all the screams were coming from vampires but I knew it would take an army bigger than the one we had to deal with them. This small bunch of well-meaning soldiers could only hope to hold them off for a short time. We couldn't have been in the medical room any more than two or three minutes before Captain Stein burst through the door. He was dripping with sweat and looked like he'd been through a war, but the war was still right behind him.

'Follow me,' he ordered, 'we're getting out of here.'

'Where are the others?' I asked.

'They're dead.'

'What, all of them?'

'Almost. We'll be joining them if you don't stop asking questions. Come on!'

Captain Stein picked a hand grenade from his belt, removed the pin and threw it into the medical room. We followed Stein out of the medical room and back down the corridor, the stone floors amplifying our footsteps. The walls of the house shook as the medical room exploded with a deafening roar behind us.

As we passed the front door, it flew from its hinges and vampires started to flood in. Stein stopped to shoot at them.

'Keep going!' he shouted, 'I'll hold them off. Get to the roof.'

Agent Simpson knew this house well and led the way. She led us up a set of stairs and I heard the rattle of machine gun fire behind us. There was the sound of screaming for a few seconds, then gunfire again. The vampires were approaching but Captain Stein was managing to hold them off.

How long can he keep them downstairs?

We were led up another set of stairs, a stone spiral staircase much narrower than before. The bag on my shoulder was beginning to slip so I reached my hand back to lift it back onto my shoulder and felt a stabbing pain in the palm of my hand. I winced and realised that I had snagged it on a sharp stone sticking out of the wall. I rolled my sleeve down and held the cuff tightly over the wound, hoping to stem the bleeding while we tried to make our escape.

We pressed on and bundled through a wooden door at the top of the stairs, finding ourselves on the roof, directly below the helicopter full of troops doing their best to take down all the vampires trying to fly towards us. The combined sound of helicopter blades, gunfire and screaming vampires was almost unbearable and the downdraft from the gunship above us was making me very uneasy on my feet.

The helicopter descended and hovered just above the roof. If a gunship that size tried to land on this old house, it would surely have fallen right through it. Under the cover of gunfire, Agent Simpson, the doctor and I made a run for it and jumped aboard. Just as we were taking off, Captain Stein appeared from the door at the top of the stairs and waved for the pilot to aim his guns at the door.

A mass of vampires flew through the doorway, right into a barrage of silver bullets from the gunship. The ash from their bodies flew into the air with thousands of tiny pieces of wood and plaster. There must have been at least fifty vampires running up the stairs but the gunfire didn't stop until they were all dead.

The helicopter lifted off and the troops on board continued to defend us against the handful of vampires still buzzing around us. When there were only two left, they decided to call it quits and flew away behind Hartley House.

'Don't worry, they won't last long. Look,' Captain Stein said, and pointed towards the horizon. I gripped my bloody hand and looked up to see the sun peeking over the top of the mountains in the distance.

Part Three

Rising Sun

62
End Of Plan A

Roxy was suffering in unbelievable agony. Even though her legs were sure to grow back in a day or so, it didn't make the wounds any less painful. She wanted to stop flying to examine the severity of her wounds but she was in a race to get back to the clan before the sun rose in the sky behind her.

She had been in similar situations many times before. Fifty years ago, when attacks on the scale of the battle at Hartley House were commonplace, she had found herself leading a squad on a mission to infiltrate a building supposedly vacated by The Brotherhood. They had realised too late that it was a trap and Roxy found herself pinned in a corner with a filing cabinet crushing her right arm. Without even thinking about it, Roxy sliced off her arm and made her escape.

On that day, most of the vampires had managed to make their getaway. Now, Roxy was airborne, making her way back to her clan.

Alone.

Her squad had caused significant damage to The Brotherhood and they had displayed their new capabilities but the mission hadn't been a success. After the fight with Captain Stein, Roxy knew she wouldn't be much use as a leader without her legs so all she felt she could do was hide in a tree and watch the battle unfold.

The Brotherhood had managed to retain the doctor and now they were on their way to their regional headquarters. Long-term security of the future of the vampire race had been within their grasp and they had failed. Roxy already had a backup plan in place but she was worried about how Salazar would react to the outcome of the mission.

When the Deputy Lord Chancellor learned of the failure of their attack, he would feel the need to take action, no matter what the plan was from here on in. He would relish the opportunity to undermine Marcus' ability to lead his clan and attempt to take over. He would report back to the Lord Chancellor in the least flattering way possible.

Roxy saw her destination: a deep, dark narrow valley ahead of her. The home of her clan rarely saw a speck of sunlight. The ideal place to hide away from the human world and plan their downfall. She flew over the edge of the valley just in time to avoid the day's first rays of sunlight.

Huge thick wooden doors opened out onto a small ledge at the bottom of the valley. Two of her brothers were standing on the ledge, looking out for any late-comers before the sun rose completely in the sky and the doors were firmly locked until dusk.

Roxy hit the ledge in a heap, screaming in agony as the pain of landing on her bloody stumps shot through her hips and into her body. The two vampires standing guard ran over to her and picked her up. They carried her inside the clan's lair and locked the doors behind them. Marcus and Salazar were standing in the main hall, eagerly awaiting the arrival of a victorious squad with Doctor Owen in tow.

They were understandably disappointed to discover Roxy wounded and alone.

'What happened?' asked Salazar, immediately trying to assert his authority on the situation. Roxy ignored Salazar's question. Her eyes met with Marcus's and she could tell from the look on his face that he was only concerned about her well-being.

'What happened to you? Are you okay?' he asked.

Roxy decided to answer her immediate boss. 'We killed almost all of the soldiers. I got in a fight with the squad captain and was forced to do this to myself to stay alive.'

'You did this to yourself?' Salazar exclaimed. His face was filled with disgust and disbelief. Roxy and Marcus shared a look that told each other they both knew that he had never fought in a battle for his race or put his life on the line for one of his brothers.

'I was cut with a silver sword,' she said, 'I had to remove my legs before the burning spread all over my body.'

Salazar didn't take long to get to the point. He had obviously spent far too long pretending to care about Roxy. 'What about the doctor?'

'There were two helicopters. One was taken out by our brother on the inside but they managed to get the doctor out in the other one.'

'I thought you said you killed all of the soldiers?'

'She said almost all of them,' said Marcus. Salazar immediately turned round and squared up to him.

'What are you doing here, Marcus? I thought you were the leader of this clan?'

'I am the leader of this clan,' Marcus protested, 'Don't worry, we have this under control.'

Salazar pointed at the mutilated body of Roxy. 'You call that under control? Look at the state of her, there's only half of her body left and she's the only one that survived.'

'You don't understand,' said Roxy, doing little to disguise her frustration at Salazar's methods, 'We have a backup plan.'

'I don't care about your backup plan. This clan is not being managed effectively so I am assuming control, effective immediately. Get her bandaged up and meet me in the dining hall. I am going to report back to the Lord Chancellor.'

Marcus was fuming and started to pace backwards and forwards, struggling to contain his anger. 'Luca, wait. There's no need for this,' he pleaded, 'Trust me, we will have the doctor back by the end of the day.'

Salazar stared straight into Marcus' eyes. 'Damn right you will, Marcus. I'm going to make sure of that. Excuse me,' he said and turned to leave, taking his mobile phone out of his jacket pocket.

Marcus leaned down to examine Roxy's body. Blood was still dripping from the wounds, just like Marcus's power over his clan was ebbing away.

'You can't let him do this,' she said, 'He's going to ruin everything. I know what you're thinking of doing. I can't see any other course of action.'

'How will we explain it?' he asked.

'We'll think of something but we can't let him get away with this,' she said as she lifted her pistol and handed it to Marcus, 'Do it. It's loaded with silver bullets. You and I are finished anyway; just don't let this bastard screw everything up that we've worked for.'

He got to his feet and followed Salazar into the dining hall, where his six protectors were standing to attention. Roxy heard a succession of loud bangs and bright flashes lighted up the darkness in the lair. Marcus quickly emerged from the dining hall.

'He wasn't expecting it, was he?' she said.

'Not at all,' Marcus said, 'As I suspected, he wasn't even trying to read our thoughts and his squad was weak.'

'We're all better off without him,' said Roxy, 'you've just got to convince the Lord Chancellor of that.'

'That'll be easier if plan B is a success,' he said as he lifted Roxy to carry her to the medical room.

63
Skinner

Another soldier finishing the night shift, another mobile phone taped to the back of his desk drawer.

Another vampire infiltrator at the regional headquarters of The Brotherhood.

Private Skinner had been working in the communications room and heard all the details of the attack on Hartley House. Private Lambert had done a good job but unfortunately the mission had not been completed. He had taken out one of the gunships and allowed a large squad of his brothers and sisters to almost completely wipe out an outpost.

But the primary target had escaped. The attack was all for nothing. His brothers and sisters had died for nothing. Private Skinner knew that now would be his time to join the fight.

Private Skinner called Roxy and she barked at him before he had the chance to say anything.

'Where is the target?' she asked, her voice laced with anger and pain.

'On his way here. The helicopter is about twenty minutes away,' he replied.

'You know what you need to do. Our cause depends on you now.'

'I understand. Is everything okay?' he asked, but didn't receive an answer. The line clicked and she was gone. Private Skinner turned his phone off and returned it to its hiding place.

Our cause depends on you.

Skinner was nervous and excited. He had trained for this moment for a long time. He was going to come face to face with the doctor. The primary target. He must not fail.

He already had his orders from The Brotherhood. He was part of the disposal team who took care of bodies that had been bitten or infected. The recovered bodies provided Private Skinner with all the human blood he needed to keep him going. He had never killed a human or fed on the blood of the living.

After a twelve hour shift, he felt the familiar pain in his stomach. He grabbed his stomach with both hands and sat down. His face contorted with agony and he fought against the hunger. The almost uncontrollable desire to feed on human flesh and blood.

The door opened and his room-mate, Private O'Brien, ran into the room, wiping shaving foam off his face with a towel. 'Damn it, I'm late again!' he cursed.

Skinner had got to know Private O'Brien well over the last two years. They worked opposite shifts and rarely saw each other, but when they did they got on like a house on fire.

O'Brien looked at his room-mate, who was still doubled over on the side of his bed. 'Hey bud, are you okay?'

'Just a bit of indigestion.'

'Too right. It was that dinner last night. I've had dodgy guts all day.'

'Yes, that must be it,' said Private Skinner as he struggled to his feet.

64
Regeneration

Roxy hung up and Marcus took the phone out of her hand. She was lying on a metal operating table, with a team of her brothers and sisters clad in medical robes leaning over her mutilated body, preparing it for regeneration.

Two of her brothers lifted her body off the treatment table and carried her over to a small bath. They sat her down on a moulded seat on the edge of the bath and let her stumps hang down. One of her sisters picked up a hose that was hanging in a long loop on the wall, placed the end in the bath and turned a tap on the wall.

Within a few seconds, cool, dark blood started to pour from the hose into the bath, covering what remained of Roxy's legs. The sticky blood worked its way up to Roxy's hips and stopped. The medical staff cleaned themselves up and threw their blood-soaked robes in a basket that was taken away by a servant. As they left, one of them turned to Roxy. 'You'll be okay but try to rest. Conserve your energy. We'll be back to check on you in an hour.'

'Thank you very much,' she said, her voice conveying a mixture of relief, disappointment and exhaustion.

Only Marcus remained in the room. 'How do you feel, Roxy?'

'I've felt worse,' she said, 'I've been in worse scrapes than this.'

'Yes you have, haven't you? What was the news?'

'It was another one of our insiders. He's going to make sure all of the bodies make it through the recovery process without being treated.'

'So plan B is a go?'

'Yes sir. One hundred percent.'

65
Arrival

An impressive formation of clouds hung above us in the blood red sky as the helicopter touched down. It was just after seven AM and we found ourselves on a landing pad on the top of a hill.

I looked around and saw a massive arsenal of military hardware. There was another gunship like the one that had picked us up from Hartley House and a wide range of other vehicles. Whoever The Brotherhood were, they were obviously well-funded but from what I'd seen in the last few hours, they could do with more experience in the field. They were well-trained to act like a military outfit but they had failed to effectively deal with the attack.

I saw a squad of soldiers running towards the other gunship. They piled in and it lifted off, heading in the direction that we had just come from.

'What's going on there?' I asked Captain Stein.

'That's the recovery team,' he replied, 'Now the sun's up, they're going back to Hartley House to clean up the mess before anyone finds out. They've got a lot of work to do today.'

A squad of soldiers marched up a long ramp leading down into the mountain. A burly man in uniform, Commander North, led the squad, shouting 'Left! Left! Left, right, left!' and the soldiers all marched in time, their thundering footsteps breaking the silence that was left behind once the helicopter had been shut down.

They reached the landing pad and surrounded the helicopter, their hands resting on their guns but not aiming at us. I could see they were ready to blow away anything that looked like a vampire: it was written in the concentration on their faces. I wondered how many of these soldiers had seen as much action as we had seen in the last twenty four hours.

Not many, I bet.

Captain Stein got out of the helicopter and saluted Commander North. 'Welcome home,' said the commander.

'Thank you, sir. It's unfortunate there aren't more of us.'

'You've got the doctor, that's what matters. Good job, Captain.'

I had been hoping the regional headquarters would have been run by someone with a bit more sympathy but it appeared to me that Captain Stein and Commander North were crafted from the same mould.

Agent Simpson and I got out of the helicopter behind Doctor Owen. Commander North took one look at me and turned to Captain Stein. 'Who the hell is this sorry looking son of a bitch? He looks like he's on his last legs,' he said as though I wasn't there.

'This is Detective Tom Ryder,' he said.

'A cop?' he said, continuing to ignore me.

'Yes. His work helped us to track down Doctor Owen.'

Commander North moved over to me. We shook hands and the bandage on my neck must have caught his eye. 'Jesus Christ, he's been bitten. I hope you know what you're doing, Captain.'

'Yes sir,' said Captain Stein, 'the Doctor is going to work with Detective Ryder. We hope this opportunity will present us with the data he needs to finish his work.'

'I hope you mean the primary treatment, Captain.'

'Of course, sir.'

'He's your responsibility, Captain,' said Commander North, then looked me in the eye, 'Son, if you start trying to eat my men, I'll put you down in the blink of an eye. Got it?'

'I'll try my best not to.' I said dourly.

The squad led us down the ramp towards the heart of the regional headquarters. As we descended, I saw more heavy military equipment including a huge array of firepower: cannons, racks of rifles and crates marked 'explosive'. Most of the vehicles looked clean and new.

Has any of this equipment ever been used? Would any of these soldiers know what to do with it if there was an attack on the base?

'How are The Brotherhood funded?' I asked Agent Simpson.

'How do you think?'

'The government?' I speculated

'It's bigger than that. The influence of the vampire community stretches all over the world.'

'So there *is* a link with the World Health Organisation? Once this all kicked off, I assumed it was a lie to get us to work together.' I said.

'No, not at all. You'd be surprised at the other problems we have to deal with.'

'One surprise is quite enough for now.' As far as I was concerned, the other problems of the World Health Organisation could wait a little longer. I didn't want to think about all the other monsters out there in the world that until now I thought existed only in the realms of fiction.

We were marched down long corridors, past many doors into the heart of the base. The place wasn't decorated at all. The walls were bare grey concrete and there were no furnishings or signs anywhere. I wondered how long The Brotherhood had been based at this location: it felt like they could leave at any time and leave no trace at all. After seeing the attack on Hartley House, I could appreciate the need for immediate evacuation.

We were led through one of the blank doors into a cold, empty room. Commander North moved to the front of the crowd and everyone else in the room faced him, awaiting his address.

'I would like to start off by welcoming the newcomers to our outpost. Some of you already know Agent Simpson and I'm sure you are all aware of Doctor Owen's work.'

He turned to me. 'Detective Ryder here was instrumental in rescuing the doctor from the hands of our enemies. I would like to thank him on behalf of The Brotherhood for all his hard work. Unfortunately for him, he was bitten in the course of his investigation.'

No sooner had the words left his lips than all the soldiers in the room turned to each other, murmuring in hushed voices and firing cautionary glances in my direction.

'Quiet please,' said Doctor Owen, 'He's okay now. I have given him a dose of the treatment I've been working on. As soon as we can have access to your medical facilities, we will continue the testing.'

Commander North looked troubled. 'I take it you gave him the secondary treatment?'

'Of course,' he said.

Secondary treatment? I thought. *What's the primary treatment?*

'A soldier will be standing by wherever he goes,' said Captain Stein, 'The chances are that he will still turn into a bloodsucker. No offence, Detective.'

'None taken.'

66
Silver Bullets

The grounds of Hartley House were filled with the smoking remnants of the battle that had raged just two hours earlier. The repercussions were being felt on both sides and would continue to be felt for a very long time after the dust had settled on these once well-manicured lawns.

The wooden towers lay in splintered bundles, the remaining ultraviolet lamps still flickering over the blood-soaked bodies of the soldiers of The Brotherhood. The grass was glazed with a heavy sprinkling of ash and silver bullets. Swords, pistols and cloaks lay where the vampires had fallen.

In the remains of the carnage, a body was stirring. One soldier had survived. Keeping pressure on the gaping wound in his neck with one hand, he used his other arm to lift a reinforced wooden support off his legs and drag himself free onto an open patch of grass.

He thought back to the battle. He had killed at least five vampires before they climbed the tower and pounced on him and his squad mate. Fortune had smiled on him though. Just as a vampire had pinned him down and sunk its teeth into his neck, the vampires at the bottom of the tower had managed to loosen the tower from its foundations. The vampire let go and they all fell to the ground.

Then a thought occurred to the soldier. *What happened to the vampire?*

The soldier felt a powerful blast of air in his face. Dust particles pelted his eyeballs and shot up his nostrils when he drew breath. With his free hand he rubbed his eyes then looked through the criss-crossing remnants of his wooden tower to see a familiar gunship approaching.

It touched down on the drive and a small squad of soldiers jumped out. He knew what their job was: to recover the bodies and take them back to the regional headquarters for safe disposal. It was safe for The Brotherhood to assume that every dead soldier at Hartley House had been bitten and was about to turn into a vampire.

This soldier was still alive and he knew the doctor had been working on a cure. He breathed a sigh of relief.

Thank God his treatment is to cure vampires rather than kill them. If it worked on that cop, it must work on me.

He looked around him and saw one soldier leading the others, shooting silver bullets into the dead bodies and the others were zipping them into body bags.

Then he heard the clunk of wood on metal. The ruins of the tower were moving. An unholy scream tore through the air and in the shade of the ruins of the tower, the vampire that had attacked the soldiers at the top of the tower wobbled to its feet. It turned and looked at the soldier, who shouted for help.

The soldier that had been shooting the dead bodies ran over and pumped the vampire's body full of bullets from his machine gun. The vampire didn't fall to the ground and die though, and the soldiers looked at each other. The soldier lying on the ground knew something was amiss.

That vampire's body is full of silver bullets but nothing happened. What's going on?

'Damn it,' said the other soldier and drew his pistol. He pulled the trigger and the target reeled backwards. The vampire hit the ground and its body slowly dissolved. The soldier holstered his pistol and moved over to the surviving soldier.

'You weren't using silver bullets,' the surviving soldier said, 'all the soldiers here are going to turn, aren't they? You're one of them!'

'That's right, soldier,' the soldier replied, then squeezed the trigger of his rifle and murdered the only human who suspected he was a vampire.

67
Prisoner

After the meeting, the doctor and I were escorted to a medical room by two soldiers sticking the barrels of their guns in our backs. My protestation was met with the comment: 'The faster you move, the less it'll hurt, asshole.'

More soldiers arrived carrying the equipment that we had managed to save from Hartley House. I wanted to ask the doctor about the primary and secondary treatments but the presence of the soldiers made me feel uneasy. Unless we were left alone or I got over my paranoia, it would be very difficult to speak candidly with someone watching me, ready to fill my body with silver bullets as soon as I started talking like a vampire.

'We've only missed one interval,' the doctor said as he looked at his watch, 'we should still have manageable data.'

It was then that I realised how much I had been through. In just over two hours I had woken up from a vampire bite induced coma, discussed my future as a human pin cushion for experimental blood treatments and narrowly escaped another battle, this time on the side of The Brotherhood against a flock of hungry vampires.

Sitting in my unmarked car drinking coffee and feeling sorry for myself felt like a lifetime ago, but it was only twenty-four hours. *I'd give anything to be back there right now*, I thought to myself.

It was at this moment I realised what a horrible person I'd been without good reason. Okay, my wife had been killed but that was five years ago and I'd caught the killer. Her killer was in jail because I'd put him there. Everything bad that had happened in those five years had been blamed on Sarah's death. The fact of the matter was that there was no one to blame anything on apart from myself.

I should have come to terms with the fact that I was on my own and I had to look after myself but I'd taken the easy route. I'd hit the bottle and the last five years were a blur. I felt like I had nothing to lose.

I had to get a grip and this was a better time than any other. Now I had everything to lose. If what the doctor was saying about me was true, then I owed it to him to stay alive. He had saved my life and now my life was in his hands.

Doctor Owen inserted a needle into a vein in my arm and took his sample. I winced and wondered how long it would take for me to get used to the injections. 'How long will we be here for?' I asked him.

'They'll probably keep us here for a while. The medical facilities are adequate and the outpost seems to be secure.' Doctor Owen seemed to have more faith in The Brotherhood than I did.

'You haven't been here before then?' I asked, 'I assumed you followed these guys around and did all of their research for them.'

'No, not at all,' he said, 'until now I've done all my work at Mantek. The turning point was when I made a breakthrough with the secondary treatment. I wasn't expecting to reach that stage for another two or three weeks. Now that the research is out in the open, so to speak, only now is it necessary to continue the research behind closed doors.'

Looking around at all of the equipment, I realised I hadn't seen any living quarters since we'd arrived. I turned to the one of the soldiers watching over us. 'Where are we supposed to sleep?'

'You've both got rooms,' he said. 'They're across the hall. We'll make sure you get all your meals, everything you need. There's no need for you to leave this level.'

'What about…' I started.

'You don't understand,' the doctor said to me, 'they won't let us leave here.'

'Why?'

'Because you've been bitten. They have to isolate you. Why do you think we were marched down here so quickly?'

The horrible reality of my future began to dawn on me. I hadn't known what to expect but for some reason I didn't think I would be locked away in a concrete bunker until the day I die.

'So I'm a prisoner here? For the rest of my life?' I asked, with desperation causing my voice to crack.

'There's only one way out of here, Detective,' said the solider.

'That's if I find a permanent cure,' the doctor said but I suspected the soldier would have finished the sentence in a different way if he'd been given the chance.

'Well we'd better get cracking then,' I said. I tried to do my best to sound upbeat. There was no point in throwing a fit. I was down here and we may as well do our best to make the most of it.

'Okay,' said the doctor, 'tell me how you feel now.'

'A little tired but other than that, I feel fine. If I start to turn, what should I expect? Do my teeth get longer? When do I start flying?'

'I've been thinking about this,' he said, 'All vampires have their differences but they all have to feed after being reborn. One of the first symptoms you can expect is an insatiable hunger, like nothing you've ever felt before.'

'For human flesh?' I asked.

'For blood, more specifically. Vampires crave human blood because theirs is deficient in a number of ways.'

'Like what?' I was no scientist but I had to find out all of the details. If something unnatural was going on in my body, I wanted to know everything.

'The energy needed to sustain the undead life of a vampire is considerably more than the energy a human needs. If a vampire sustains an injury, it will heal itself very quickly, which requires an incredible amount of energy. The only way is to absorb more red blood cells into the body.'

I realised my hand had stopped hurting where it had been cut during the escape from Hartley House. I opened it and looked at my palm, expecting to see the bloody wound.

There was nothing. There was no trace of the wound at all. I held up my hand. 'I cut this hand just before we got on the helicopter, now it's completely healed.'

Doctor Owen took my hand in his for a closer look. 'Very interesting,' he said, 'one attribute has shown itself but there are no other obvious signs that you have been infected.'

He removed the bandage from my neck and held a small mirror up for me to look into. 'Look,' he said, 'your bite mark has gone as well.'

This made me feel very uneasy. My body thought I was a vampire and was starting to act like one. My thoughts turned to my impending desire to drink human blood.

'How do vampires choose their victims?'

'Vampires must feed on humans with the same blood type as them. Experienced vampires seem to be able to tell what blood type humans have. A new vampire will kill as many humans as it can before finding the correct blood type.

'Needless to say, vampires with rare blood types don't tend to last very long. For what it's worth, I tested your blood type earlier and you've got a very common blood type, O positive. If you start to feel hungry, you won't have to kill very many people to find a match.'

'Thanks, Doc. That's comforting.'

68
Questions

Under the circumstances, I seemed to be getting on pretty well with Doctor Owen. He had me hooked up to various machines that beeped every few seconds and kept prodding and poking me but even so, with the exception of Agent Simpson, he was the only one treating me as if I was human.

I hoped I had enough blood left because he was taking a hell of a lot out of me and squirting it into test tubes. Everywhere I looked I could see my blood, labelled with the date and time.

He was explaining a lot to me but it surprised me how many gaps he was so far unable to fill. For example, no one knew where vampires got their powers.

How can they fly?

How do they absorb and process human blood?

Why do they have superhuman strength?

All these questions and more needed to be answered before the doctor could expect to find a cure for the virus.

'It has been very difficult to conduct these kinds of experiments. The problem is that these guys are so twitchy, they never bring back a live specimen,' he sighed.

Captain Stein walked into the room. 'What would you have my men do, Doctor? Ask them to come quietly?'

'There must be a way of capturing a vampire without killing it. Without a live specimen, my work remains in the realm of theory and speculation. That is the only reason that we know very little about vampires.'

'What about our friend here?' the Captain asked, pointing at me.

'I am getting an incredible amount of data from Detective Ryder but there's no guarantee that he'll change. For all I know, I'm just filling this lab up with clean human blood.' He was covering up the miraculous healing of my hand, which cemented my suspicion that he trusted

Captain Stein as little as I did. I lifted the bandage to my neck again before Captain Stein could notice that the wound had healed.

'This situation is tough for all of us, Doctor. We have to make do with what we've got so keep at it. I want you to present your findings to the Commander first thing tomorrow morning. Remember, he is expecting the primary treatment to be your main focus, same as me.'

'What do you mean?' he protested, 'I'm still in the data gathering stage.'

'You heard me, Doc. Give me results!' said the Captain and left the room, slamming the door behind him.

I decided to ignore the soldier standing in the corner of the room and ask the Doctor the question that had been burning in my head since we arrived.

'What are the primary and secondary treatments?'

The doctor glanced at the soldier as well and hesitated but decided to tell me anyway. He had been given one day to come up with results that were not physically possible. I suspected he was beginning to feel as much of a prisoner as I did.

'The secondary treatment is what I gave you,' he started, 'The whole idea behind the secondary treatment is to remove the effects of the virus and to stop it taking over all bodily functions. This may then lead to a treatment that could reverse the rebirth process: to return vampires to their natural human state.'

'So the secondary treatment is a cure?'

'Eventually it will be, yes.'

'And the primary treatment?' I asked.

'To develop a treatment that will cause a violent chemical reaction with the virus. The primary treatment will kill any vampire it is given to. The Brotherhood would rather have a poison than a remedy. They seem to think it will be easier to develop and deploy a formula that will kill all vampires without affecting humans.'

'Are they right?'

'Probably, but there's no way Captain Stein or Commander North know anything about this research on a scientific level. They have no time for development and experiments. All they want to see are results but anyone who has worked in my field knows that once you start, tangible results may be years away, even for the primary treatment. Shouting louder won't lead to results any sooner.

'The secondary treatment would be the only true way of ridding vampires from this world. By immunising everyone at birth, within a generation there would be no vampires.'

To me, it sounded like an ideal solution. A vaccination for all would mean no more vampire rebirths and all the undead brothers and sisters could be returned to their natural state and start to live their human lives again.

I could see why this plan didn't appeal to certain members of The Brotherhood. They weren't exactly the most sophisticated bunch of people I had ever met. They had brand new expensive military hardware up to their ears and you can be damn sure they were itching to use it.

'Hang on a minute, there's a problem here,' I said as something occurred to me, 'Even if you could develop a vaccine, how would you distribute it? As soon as word got out, the vampires would just launch another massive attack and destroy the stock of any vaccine you had.'

'I'm aware of this,' said the doctor, 'and if you can think of a way to do it, make sure you let me know.'

It was at this moment that I realised my job was to sit in this lab with a scientist who was learning everything from scratch. I felt like the zombie guinea pig from a horror movie I watched late one night while struggling to sleep. I guess I had to be happy that I hadn't been chained to the walls. Not yet, anyway.

'What about Doctor Forrest?' I asked.

'What about him?'

'How is he involved in all of this?'

'You mean does he know more about it than I do?' the doctor asked with a wry smile on his face. He was right though, that was exactly what I meant. I was sure Doctor Owen would forgive me for wanting to have as many experts around me as possible.

'You may be right,' I said, 'but can he help us?'

'He's a very old man,' said Doctor Owen, 'he's been working on this pretty much his whole life without getting very far. Then we managed to make the breakthrough recently and came up with the experimental vaccine that I gave to you. After that he disappeared and I haven't seen him for over a week. He goes AWOL from time to time so I just assumed he took a break.'

'So now you think they've got him?' I asked.

'Well he's been a member of The Brotherhood for all of his life. He's not here and no one's heard from him. All we can do is assume that he's either gone into hiding or the vampires have him.'

'Either way, you're not going to see him again, are you?'

'We should continue our work as if he's not going to be found.'

69
Bodies

The sun was high in the sky as the recovery crew's gunship landed at the regional headquarters, loaded with the dead bodies from Hartley House. A large white flatbed buggy whizzed up the ramp and stopped at the back of the helicopter. The recovery crew disembarked and started to transfer the body bags onto the buggy, some of which were tagged with red labels, some with blue labels.

The red-labelled bags contained soldiers that had been bitten by vampires. There were twelve of them. The process usually followed by the recovery crew is to shoot the infected bodies with silver bullets, bag them up, take them back to base and either let the bodies burn when they turn into vampires or slice them up to provide Doctor Owen with more samples to use in his experiments.

This time it was different. The bodies had been shot with regular bullets. The bodies in the red-labelled bags were starting to turn.

A member of the recovery crew was a vampire, but not a vampire in the way The Brotherhood knew. This vampire could withstand direct sunlight without incurring instant sunburn. Ash didn't drip from his open sores. He was by no means a typical vampire and he wasn't the only one.

It was Mother Nature's love of diversity that helped the vampires infiltrate many levels of human society and it was the stereotypical view of vampires held by humans and the ignorance of The Brotherhood that allowed them to go unnoticed.

Once the buggy was full, the driver took it back down the ramp towards the morgue, deep in the heart of the base.

70
Enter The Angel

Like an angel sent from heaven to bring light into my life deep within this stone fortress, Agent Simpson glided into the lab holding three cups of coffee.

'I thought you could both do with a break,' she said.

We both extended our eternal gratitude but the soldier standing guard in the corner was put out. 'Hey, what about me?' he protested.

'Get your own,' we all said in unison. A brief silent pause was quickly filled with laughter at the guard's expense, who started to look less menacing and headed for the door.

'Screw you guys, I'm going for a break,' he announced and shouted to a colleague down the corridor as he opened the door, 'Hey Steve, keep an eye on this lot in here for a minute.'

With that, the three of us were left without a chaperone.

'So how are you two doing?' Agent Simpson asked.

'Pretty good,' I said, 'the doc was just filling me in on a few more details. There's one thing I don't really understand though.'

'What's that?'

'Why is all of this happening now? If vampires and humans have been at each other's throats, no pun intended, for the whole of eternity, why have things started to get out of hand now?'

Doctor Owen piped up. 'We reached a critical stage in the development of the treatment.'

'Primary or secondary?' I asked.

'Primary.'

'I thought you weren't working on it.'

'Of course we are. The primary treatment is what we're paid to work on but we kept working on the secondary treatment in the background.'

'How do you keep working on both at the same time?'

'The Brotherhood believe whatever we tell them. We are the scientific experts. About a year ago, we told Captain Stein that the next phase would take twelve months to complete, but we were only a couple of months away from completion. That bought us the time we needed to develop the secondary treatment on the side. If we hadn't, you'd be in a lot of trouble.'

'Well I thank you for that,' I said, contemplating the choices that could have made the difference between my death and the state of delayed death that I found myself in. 'So where are you up to with the primary treatment?'

'The primary treatment is nearing completion. We have successfully developed a compound that breaks down infected blood much quicker than silver. The problem that faces us in the next phase is to find an application for the compound that is easily distributed so The Brotherhood don't have to kill every vampire one by one.'

'The same problem you have with the secondary treatment.'

'Exactly. Our plan was to bring development of the secondary treatment to the same level as the primary then switch the compounds before distribution so the vampires will be cured rather than killed, but we've run into more problems with the secondary treatment.'

'It only works for a limited time.'

'Correct. At the moment, it's only a treatment, not a cure. It's going to become more and more difficult to work towards a cure with The Brotherhood breathing down our necks here.'

We all looked at each other with the same thoughts in mind but chose not to voice them. For now.

71
Alone In The Morgue

Private Skinner had a lot of work to do. He stood alone in the morgue, looking down on a large pile of body bags. The leftovers from the battle of Hartley House.

This delivery was the largest Private Skinner had ever seen. The attack had been unprecedented in recent history and from the comments of the staff at the base and the recovery crew as they made the drop-off, everyone was still reeling from it. The vampires had now set the standard. Their numbers were significantly greater than The Brotherhood had anticipated. The humans would have to wake up to the threat the vampires imposed or they would leave themselves wide open to greater defeats.

Private Skinner's usual job was to arrange the bodies of the fallen soldiers into two sections: bitten and just plain dead. For the bodies that had been bitten by vampires, he had to remove their dog tags and make a note of who they were before the silver bullets they had been treated with caused their bodies to burn when they turned.

Only this time it would be different: they had been shot with regular bullets. No one ever checked what type of bullets the recovery crew used. Once a soldier had gone through the acceptance process, it was assumed they were human. There were never any follow-up tests.

Private Skinner's orders were to let the new-born vampires loose into the headquarters and allow them to run amok, killing as many members of The Brotherhood as possible.

This would cause a distraction that would allow him to capture the doctor and make their escape. He had a helicopter fuelled and waiting on the tarmac many floors above.

There had never been a successful attack on such a heavily guarded compound as this, but everything so far had been surprisingly easy. It made Private Skinner wonder why they hadn't tried it before.

Then he realised all the work that had gone into getting him to join The Brotherhood and the necessity of the situation he found himself in. He had never known a mission to be carried out with so much urgency.

He had to return the doctor to his brothers and sisters. If he didn't, Doctor Owen would continue his work and eventually discover a way of ridding his brothers and sisters from the world. Private Skinner knew Roxy wouldn't allow that to happen and he wanted to be the one to make a difference.

But for now, Private Skinner was hungry. He had never fed on the blood of live humans. He hadn't been able to bring himself to do it, which is why he was happy to take care of the bodies in the morgue.

His canine teeth shifted in their sockets as he approached the pile of dead human bodies.

72
Doctor Forrest

Doctor Owen's mobile phone rang and he looked at the screen before answering.

'Oh my God,' he exclaimed, 'it's Doctor Forrest.'

Agent Simpson's eyes widened and she had an expression on her face that was familiar to me. It was the look of someone who has just been informed that a missing loved one has been found. As a detective, it was very rare to recover a missing person, especially in this city, but the loved ones of a missing person always have the same expression of surprise and happiness that is unforgettable.

We stood in anxious silence as the doctors exchanged words.

'Hello?' said Doctor Owen, 'Yes, it's good to hear from you. How are you? Good. Where are you? Why not? I've got another subject here. He's responding well to the secondary treatment. Yes, you're absolutely right. I'll inform The Brotherhood, then we'll recover the items and come and find you. What? Why? I don't understand. Well, if you say so but it's going to be very difficult. Okay, keep in touch. Bye.'

He had barely hung up when Agent Simpson spoke up. 'What did he say?'

Doctor Owen looked very confused. 'He said he's safe and well but he wouldn't say where he was. He suspected someone might have been listening and he doesn't want to be found.

'He said we have to recover our notes and samples from the labs around the city, all the stuff that wasn't destroyed in the attack on Mantek. He has a plan for distribution. He didn't say what it was but there's something I don't understand. He wants us to recover everything without the help of The Brotherhood. We can't let them know he has contacted us.'

'That's very strange,' said Agent Simpson, 'he's been a member of The Brotherhood all of his life. So have you, Doctor.'

'Yes, he said he didn't trust them any more. He said the plan is simple and we can achieve everything without their help if we can get out of here.'

I was caught in the middle of a situation I was struggling to understand but I felt I had to say something. 'Well Doc, wherever you go, I go. How the hell are we going to get out of here?'

My question was met with blank looks.

'Do you think we can trust the doctor?' Agent Simpson asked. 'What reason do we have to betray The Brotherhood?'

Looks like we're going to be here for a while, I thought.

73
Call From The Boss

The next few hours passed without incident. Doctor Owen continued to take blood from my veins and we talked a lot about anything and everything. He told me all about his wife and the life they shared. I felt sorry for him. As soon as he realised his work was so crucial, they made the decision to devote their lives to the cause. I thought his wife must be an incredibly strong woman to stand by him and sacrifice the things she always wanted.

The soldier had returned from his break and in silence, we continued to attempt to formulate a plan to get out of this base but the look on Doctor Owen's face told me he was struggling to come up with options.

I had nothing. The base was heavily guarded and we were the VIPs. We couldn't even step outside the lab without attracting attention.

Agent Simpson was busy in another part of the base debriefing her contacts within the World Health Organisation but she came into the lab from time to time to check up on me. I knew she felt guilty about what had happened to me but I couldn't see how the things could have turned out any differently.

I flinched as I felt a rattling in my pocket. It was my mobile phone. I had completely forgotten about making contact with the outside world. I knew exactly who the caller would be.

'Where the hell are you?' shouted Captain Nash as soon as I answered, 'you haven't turned up for work and no one's heard from you since your little car chase through downtown last night.'

I paused, not knowing where to start. How could I even begin to explain what I had been through in the past twenty-four hours?

'Well?' the Captain continued angrily, 'Get your ass down here now or you're fired! I've got the doctor's wife here but no one to question her.'

'I can't,' I protested.

'Give me one good reason why.'

'You wouldn't believe me if I told you,' I said wearily, knowing that I'd have to tell him anyway. Typical Nash, always sticking his nose in. If we didn't call in with an update every day, he thought we were bunking off.

Doctor Owen looked at me. He shrugged his shoulders and mouthed the words 'Tell him.'

'Try me,' Captain Nash snapped.

'Okay,' I said and took a deep breath, 'the murder you sent me to investigate was committed by a vampire. Mantek pharmaceuticals are working with an ancient group of vampire hunters called The Brotherhood to produce a vaccine that will rid the world of vampires. The vampires have taken exception to that plan and are fighting back.'

'What the hell are you talking about, Detective?' he shouted, 'Do you think I was born yesterday?'

'Wait, I haven't finished,' I continued, 'Both myself and Doctor Owen, who was missing until he was rescued in the helicopter attack on the Expressway yesterday, are now at The Brotherhood's regional headquarters. I am being experimented on because I was bitten by a vampire last night and they think I'm now the chosen one that will allow them to produce the vaccination they need to rid the world of vampires forever. I'll call you back with an update in twenty four hours unless I've turned into a vampire, then I won't be contactable for the rest of my undead life.'

Doctor Owen smiled at me as Captain Nash muttered something and hung up on me. 'What did he say to that?' asked the doctor.

'He told me that I'm a disgusting drunk and I should take the rest of the week off to sober up,' I said.

'Are you an alcoholic?' asked the Doctor. He looked concerned but I didn't know if that was because he had my welfare in mind or if it was because it might screw up his experiments.

'Not any more,' I said.

'How long have you been dry?'

'Nine days.'

'How is being sober treating you?'

'To be honest, I haven't thought about it until now. I've got more important things to worry about now.'

'Indeed you have, Detective. I must say that's a very good attitude.'

'He mentioned your wife as well. Sounds like they're holding her indefinitely until I go back there to talk to her.'

'Don't worry about her,' he said, 'I'll let the Captain know and he'll send someone along to pick her up.'

The door burst open and Agent Simpson ran through, looking very worried.

'What's wrong?' I asked.

'It's Captain Stein. He's on his way down here and he's not alone.'

'What does he want?' asked the doctor.

'I don't know but he looks very pissed off.'

74
Too Close

Captain Nash slammed the phone down and shook his head. It wasn't as if he couldn't believe what Detective Ryder had just told him, the fact of the matter was that he had known exactly what was going on since the attack on Mantek. He just felt sorry for Ryder.

Don't let an outsider take this investigation, they had said. *Put one of your men on the case, someone who won't be missed if he gets too close.*

Ryder had got far too close and now he was in the middle of something that Nash had managed to keep hidden from outsiders within the police department for a long time but when this case came along, Ryder was all he had.

The poor, pathetic drunk. He gets results but no one round here likes him and no one will ask any questions if something happens to him.

Emily Owen was being held in a cell on her own and now that he had an update from Ryder to keep his superiors quiet for another few hours, Nash's job was to baby-sit the doctor's wife. She was a pleasant enough woman but she wasn't in the mood for talking. Nash had tried all he could to break her down but he didn't have much to threaten her with. He wasn't planning to tell her The Brotherhood were keeping her husband safe. He'd let her sit in her cell and worry for another few hours then try talking to her again.

The vampires would surely know that the doctor had been safely returned to The Brotherhood and they were certain to attempt to recover his wife to use as leverage. Captain Nash knew he had to inform his brothers and sisters of the current status.

He took his keys out of his pocket and unlocked the bottom drawer under his desk. He fished around under a stack of papers for a mobile phone that he hadn't used for a long time. He turned the phone on and dialled a number that was etched into his mind. A familiar voice answered.

'Hi Roxy,' said Captain Nash.

'Nash, what is it?' snapped Roxy. *Always straight to the point.*

'The Brotherhood have Doctor Owen in their custody.'

'I know. Anything else?'

'I have his wife. She's being held at the station. She'll be released tomorrow unless we can find a reason to keep her here. I'm trying my best but in case she gets out…'

'That's good news, but don't concern yourself with the details of her release. I will send one of my men down to get her.'

'I won't be able to release her to a stranger.'

'You misunderstand me. I will send someone down to get her. You do not have to do anything.'

75
Blood Tests

I heard the footsteps of the squad marching down the corridor outside the lab. Captain Stein led the way, almost knocking the door off its hinges as he barged into the makeshift lab. A line of eight unarmed soldiers followed him and lined up next to each other. More soldiers walked through the doors, their rifles trained on the procession that had just appeared.

My instincts told me this would end badly. I'd only known Captain Stein for a matter of hours and I'd already worked out that subtlety and tact were not his forte. This was a situation that could almost certainly have been handled more appropriately.

'What is the meaning of this?' demanded Doctor Owen.

Stein's face had his determination written all over it. 'In the attack on Hartley House, the first helicopter was destroyed by an infiltrator. A vampire got past our security checks so we're taking steps to increase the security of the base.

'I've decided that we can't take any more risks. Everyone who leaves the base must be checked on re-entry. These men were on the recovery team that brought the bodies of the dead soldiers back from Hartley House this morning so they must be tested.'

'How are you going to do that?' the doctor asked.

'You tell me,' said Captain Stein, 'you're the expert.'

Doctor Owen knew that answer was coming. He thought to himself for a moment and came up with a plan.

'Okay, I know what we can do. We all know that vampires have an adverse reaction to silver,' he started, 'We take a blood sample from everyone and test its reaction with silver. If the blood burns then we know it belongs to a vampire. Simple as that.'

'Very good, Doctor. What are you waiting for? Start the tests,' ordered Captain Stein.

The doctor handed a small metal tray to me and asked me to help him. I held the tray for him as he lined up eight syringes and eight petri dishes. I followed him as he approached one of the armed soldiers.

'Hand me your gun,' he ordered.

The soldier looked at Captain Stein, who nodded to him. 'Do it, soldier. You heard the man.'

He handed the rifle over to the doctor, who removed the clip and ejected eight silver bullets, placing one in each of the Petri dishes. He then made his way over to the line of eight unarmed soldiers.

'Roll up your sleeves. All of you.' They all complied with his order.

I could see the doctor was relishing this brief period of authority. He picked up a syringe and grabbed the first soldier's arm, tapping the top of his forearm to bring the veins to the surface of the skin.

'Just relax,' he said, 'If you're not a bloodsucker, you've got nothing to worry about.'

Before he finished his sentence, the needle was in the soldier's arm, drawing blood from his vein. The doctor removed the syringe and turned towards me. He looked me in the eye with the syringe poised over the petri dish.

Even if this soldier is a vampire, what will happen to him? Will the armed soldiers immediately blow him away or will he be locked away and prodded like me? Will he suddenly turn and start sucking our blood?

Very slowly, he pressed the plunger and the blood poured over the silver bullet into the petri dish.

Nothing happened.

'Looks like you're all clear, son,' announced the doctor. The soldier breathed a sigh of relief and wiped the sweat from his brow. It was at this point that I realised the soldier was asking himself the same question I had been asking myself all day.

How do you know if you are a vampire?

I felt no different than I usually did but here I was, the bookie's favourite to be feeding on human flesh by the end of the week. Or maybe even the end of the day.

As the doctor was taking a blood sample from the second nervous, sweaty soldier, I cast my eyes across the other six. They all had similar looks on their faces and moved around nervously on the spot, not knowing where to put their hands.

Apart from one.

The fourth soldier in line stood perfectly still. It probably meant nothing but he was conspicuous by his lack of reaction. Something was nagging in the back of my mind, telling me this soldier wasn't to be trusted. It was more than a cop's hunch, something I had absolute certainty of but I couldn't explain the reason why.

'Clear.'

The second soldier left the line-up of suspects and joined his other colleague behind the armed soldiers. As I suspected, the third soldier was clear as well and the doctor moved to the odd-looking one. He flinched just like the others when the doctor stuck the syringe in his arm to take his blood.

The doctor moved over to me and pressed the plunger on the syringe. The soldier's blood poured onto the silver bullet lying in the petri dish. As soon as the blood touched the bullet, a small plume of smoke began to rise and flecks of ash settled in the dish. Everyone backed away from the soldier very quickly, apart from the armed men who moved a step closer to him.

Captain Stein moved forward. 'So it was you, son. How did you make it through the trials? How many more vampires are there in the base?'

'Fuck you, Captain,' the vampire soldier said, 'my job here is done.'

Stein looked at the men who had passed the blood test. 'Hold him.'

They quickly approached the soldier, one grabbing each arm and the other holding his legs together so he couldn't move. Stein punched him hard in the face, right on the end of his nose. As the soldier's body slumped into unconsciousness, Stein grabbed him by his shirt collar and threw him onto the bed. He ordered the soldiers that had been given the all clear to tie the body down.

'You asked me for a live specimen. There it is. Now finish testing these guys and show me some real results.'

76
Discoveries

Doctor Owen quickly finished testing the blood of the four remaining soldiers. My mind had told me they weren't vampires and I was right. Our focus then turned to the unconscious vampire tied to the bed. The doctor filled a syringe with anaesthetic and injected it into the vampire's arm.

'I'll need your help,' the doctor said to me under his breath, 'this isn't going to be easy.'

'Why?' I asked, 'Haven't you done experiments like this a hundred times before?'

'I've performed autopsies and dissected plenty of infected animals but this is going to be very delicate. I need to examine the inner workings of his body in as much detail as possible without killing him but remember I'm a scientist, not a surgeon. If he dies, his body will probably turn to ash and I've no idea what Captain Stein will do next. We also need to make sure the soldier doesn't wake up.'

For the second time today, the doctor appeared to not know what he was doing but like before, he was doing a good job of hiding this fact from everyone apart from me. He was quick to come up with a plan of action whenever necessary but I now realised that nothing we were doing had ever been attempted before.

Every time he performed an experiment, he was setting a precedent, like watching Walton and Cockcroft split the atom or being there under the tree to see the apple bounce off Newton's head.

'You've already pumped him full of anaesthetic. What's the problem?' I asked.

'I've no idea what effect the anaesthetic will have, if any. For all I know, he's still unconscious from Stein's punch in the face. I've given him enough to keep a human out for four or five hours but we need to keep watching him for movement, in case he wakes up.'

The doctor had a point. After seeing Officer Myers leap from one vehicle to another and punch through the windscreen of my car, it occurred to me that the straps holding the soldier down might not keep him down for long.

I held the metal tray for the doctor again as he filled it with medical instruments. 'Why me? Why don't you get one of these guys to help out? Some of them must be trained medics.'

'You're the only one I trust,' said Doctor Owen, 'Agent Simpson, I need your help as well.'

She walked over to the doctor, who handed her a video camera. 'I need you to film everything. It's going to be fairly gruesome so if you're squeamish and have to look away, just make sure you keep the camera pointing at what I'm doing. Blood doesn't make you faint, does it?'

'Not at all, I've seen far worse things in my time,' she said, looking a little worried.

'Good. Let's get started,' Captain Stein shouted, and clapped his hands together very loudly.

I stood next to the soldier's perfectly still body, flanked by Doctor Owen and Agent Simpson. I felt like they were the only allies I had in a base that was supposedly the home of the good guys.

I agreed with the doctor: I didn't trust anyone here that was part of The Brotherhood and I was surprised Agent Simpson counted herself as one of them. She didn't seem as brainwashed as the others, maybe because she had been out there in the real world seeing how the vampire virus affects society instead of sitting in the headquarters waiting on the call to jump on a helicopter and shoot some bad guys.

She had come to tell us that Captain Stein was on his way and she had saved my life, running the risk of being thrown out of The Brotherhood or worse. I wondered if she was starting to question the legitimacy of the methods used to further their cause.

'Are we filming?' asked the doctor. Agent Simpson lifted the camera up and focused on the soldier's bare torso. She pressed the record button and gave the doctor a thumbs-up with her free hand.

'Where are you going to start?' asked Captain Stein.

'I'm going to check all the vital organs to see if there is any deterioration,' said the doctor. He was back to sounding like he knew what he was talking about. 'I suspect that vampires have some form of deficiency that necessitates the consumption of human blood. I want to see how the deficiency affects the internal organs.'

'Okay, don't let me hold you up,' said the Captain as he looked on. He was a little too eager to see the soldier's insides for my liking.

Doctor Owen started his commentary for the video camera as he pulled on his surgical gloves and waved at me to hand him a scalpel. 'I will begin by making an incision in the chest cavity to examine the stomach and intestines.'

He took the scalpel out of my hands and looked at me. The look on his face told me he had no idea what to expect. As far as anyone in the room knew, we were about to witness the very first live vampire autopsy.

Very carefully, Doctor Owen leaned over the body and pushed the scalpel into the soldier's skin just below the middle of his rib cage and started to cut him open, stopping just above his navel. Blood started to pour from the wound, which the doctor seemed be very surprised about.

'There is an incredible amount of blood in the chest cavity: possible haemorrhage in one or more of the organs.'

The blood poured out of the soldier's chest, onto the bed and started to drip onto the floor. The doctor continued, 'Subject is losing massive amounts of blood.'

'This is going to make a right mess,' Captain Stein interrupted. Doctor Owen shot a dirty look in his direction.

'If you want to help, get a bucket,' he snapped. Captain Stein did nothing. 'I'm serious. Get a bucket now! I have a theory.'

One of the armed soldiers put down his rifle, picked up a plastic basin and placed it under the bed, catching the dripping blood. At the rate the blood was gushing out of the soldier's body, it wouldn't be long until the basin filled up.

'What's the theory?' asked the Captain.

Doctor Owen was fishing around inside the dark wet chest cavity. 'All the organs feel larger than normal. I suspect they are filled with blood.'

'Why isn't that normal?'

'This man's stomach should feel like a small football, hollow and leathery on the outside. It feels more like a wet sponge, much bigger and heavier than it should be.' The doctor squeezed the soldier's stomach and commented on its quick return to a larger-than-normal size. His hands emerged, completely covered in blood.

Captain Stein was looking at the doctor in disbelief, the colour draining from his face.

'Have a go if you don't believe me,' said the doctor.

'I'll pass,' said Captain Stein, conceding that Doctor Owen knew more than he did, 'So what does that mean?'

'I suspect the virus breaks down the organ tissue. This man's body is no longer the well-organised system that we are all blessed with.

In our bodies, each organ has a purpose: one organ feeds the next in a specific order. Food reaches your stomach, which is broken down and processed through the intestines to transport energy to your muscles via the blood.

'The walls of this man's organs appear to be more permeable, meaning that blood can pass directly from one area of the body to the other, straight through the organs, bypassing the circulatory system. That will explain their incredible strength: blood can pass directly to the necessary muscles whereas our blood needs to travel through the complicated system of veins and arteries.'

'But how is the blood directed?' I asked, 'The blood is pumped around our bodies by the heart. How can a vampire's heart decide where to assign the blood?'

'One step at a time, Detective.'

'Doctor Owen,' said Agent Simpson, sounding very concerned, 'what's happening to the blood?'

The drip of blood into the basin stopped. The stream of blood from the body to the basin hung in the air, defying the laws of gravity.

Then something even more unbelievable happened.

The blood started to pour upwards, out of the basin and back into the vampire's chest cavity.

Frozen with shock, everyone in the lab watched as every drop of blood made its way from the basin under the bed back into the vampire's body. Then the level of blood in the chest cavity dropped and the open wound in the vampire's chest quickly sealed itself shut.

The doctor looked very concerned. 'The blood must be moving to an area of the body where it is needed.'

'Where?' I asked.

I looked at the soldier's face and saw his eyes open.

77
'Butcher him'

The vampire soldier's eyes darted around maniacally in their sockets then locked onto mine. He opened his mouth to reveal extended canine teeth. The muscles in his arms and legs tensed but the straps tying him down were holding him to the bed. For now.

'Jesus Christ! He's woken up already, shoot him!' Captain Stein exclaimed and the armed soldiers clicked the safety catches on their rifles.

'No, wait!' shouted the doctor as he reached across me, picked up a syringe full of anaesthetic and injected it into the soldier's neck. Within a few seconds, the soldier's eyes and mouth closed and his body lost its powerful energy.

'This is too dangerous, Doc,' said the Captain, 'if that happens again, I will shoot him.' The doctor turned to Captain Stein, ready to start an argument but soon realised that he wouldn't have a chance of winning. Instead, he turned to me once again.

'We'd better do as much as we can before he wakes up again. My original estimation of four to five hours of unconsciousness was way out. I now estimate around twenty to thirty minutes before he wakes up.'

'So what's the plan?' I asked.

The doctor thought to himself for a few moments. 'We butcher him. As fast as we can.' He turned to the soldiers. 'Gather up all the basins and buckets you can find.' They all turned to Captain Stein for guidance.

'Don't look at me,' he said, 'Do what he said. You heard him, we haven't got much time.'

Doctor Owen leaned over the body of the undead soldier with a scalpel and reopened the chest cavity. As the soldiers ran around the labs gathering together all the vessels they could find, the doctor was dipping conical flasks into the chest cavity one after another, collecting as many samples as possible, and putting corks in the tops of the flasks to stop the vampire blood making its own way out. He knew this soldier would die very soon and wanted to get as much data for further examination as possible before our time ran out.

The basins piled up on the bench next to us and the doctor ordered me to stand by and hand him a new basin for each organ that he was going to extract. I held the first basin in front of me. In one quick move, the doctor yanked the soldier's stomach out of his abdominal cavity and sliced it free from the rest of his digestive tract. It landed in my basin with a watery splat, followed by the order: 'Get ready, here comes the liver!'

For the next few minutes I managed to catch all the organs that Doctor Owen threw at me. The organs were all drenched in blood and splashed drops onto me as they landed in each basin. The doctor stopped and we both looked at the organs lined up on the bench next to us. He had extracted the stomach, liver, kidneys, intestines, heart and lungs.

'Very interesting,' he commented.

'What is it?' I asked.

'If we assume that a vampire's body turns into ash when it dies, we can therefore assume that this man is still quote-unquote alive, even though all of his vital organs are sitting over there. Look, the blood is still active.'

He was right. This was a very unsettling experience. In each of the basins, the drops of blood that had splattered around the organs were making their way back into their host. Every drop of blood was alive, with a mind of its own dictating its movements.

'What does that mean?' asked Captain Stein.

'It means that this man has no use for his internal organs. The biological processes required to sustain human life cease to be relevant once the virus has consumed the body. It is safe to assume that the muscles are still required by the limbs in order for them to function but it appears this body runs almost solely on blood. That must be why vampires feed on human blood: nothing else provides them with the sustenance their bodies need. It is as if the virus has taken control of the blood completely and is using the body as a home.

'When we saw the blood drain from the chest cavity, it must have been moving to the brain to provide the energy necessary to overcome the effects of the anaesthetic.'

Everyone in the lab stood in silence. Doctor Owen had just delivered a bombshell. As long as the human race had walked the Earth, vampires had always been the enemy and now, for the first time in recorded history, we had biological evidence of the differences between them and us. The first step on the path to rid them from our world.

Something else occurred to me. *What if vampires are the superior species? Are we trying to rid the world of the next step in human evolution?* The anatomy of a vampire seemed so much simpler, so much more elegant than that of a human body.

I looked at the body of the soldier and saw the blood start to drain away from his chest cavity. Just as it had before, the chest cavity closed like an invisible zipper was being done up.

'Doc, he's going to wake up again.'

Captain Stein picked up his gun but the doctor stopped him.

'No sense wasting another bullet,' said Doctor Owen as he picked a bullet up from the petri dishes and casually lobbed it into the soldier's wound just before it closed completely. As the soldier's eyes opened, smoke started to rise from his chest and the burning spread around the body.

The soldier screamed and tried to shake himself free. The bed rattled and he managed to rip one of the straps and release one of his arms but it was too late. As he tried to reach over to free his other arm, it turned to ash, along with the rest of his body. Within seconds, nothing was left of the soldier other than a thick layer of ash.

'Good work, Doctor,' Captain Stein conceded, 'keep at it. Looks like you've got a lot of samples to get to work on.' He marched most of the soldiers out of the lab, leaving one volunteer behind to keep an eye on us.

Doctor Owen, Agent Simpson and I looked at each other and assessed our surroundings. We were faced with a bed covered in ash from a dead vampire and a row of basins filled with live organs. The organs had not turned into ash. They looked exactly the same: fat, moist and full of vampire blood.

'Very interesting,' said Doctor Owen, 'the organs haven't died, even though the vampire's body has died.'

'What does that mean?' asked Agent Simpson.

Doctor Owen smiled. 'To be honest, I've no idea. It feels like we've discovered penicillin, cracked the human genome and discovered the triple helix all on the same day. I think we've earned a five minute break.'

We all nodded in agreement. Unfortunately, it was that very second that I felt a burning in my stomach like nothing I had ever felt before but I instinctively knew what it was. I gripped my stomach with both hands and doubled over in agony.

Like the doctor had predicted and I had feared, I was suddenly unbelievably hungry.

78
Second Thoughts

Private Skinner was shocked. Standing in the medical lab with the recovery crew, he had witnessed the death of one of his brothers, but for the first time he believed the death wasn't in vain. He had witnessed the massacre of many humans and vampires, all of them killed for no good reason that he could fathom. Every battle was a futile exercise that resulted in a pile of dead bodies without any advancement for either species.

This time the death seemed to have some value. The people doing the experiments wanted to help everyone, not just the humans. They wanted what was best for all species. Private Skinner was a sworn enemy of The Brotherhood but these people weren't like the others.

These people, Doctor Owen, Detective Ryder and Agent Simpson, weren't bloodthirsty animals. They had a measured approach towards these experiments. Not once had they mentioned the *primary treatment.*

He had only been a vampire for a relatively short time and could still remember life before his rebirth. He hadn't chosen this life. It had chosen him one drunken night when he fell over on the long walk home and passed out in the street. When he woke up in hospital he had a bandage on his neck and a splitting headache. The hunger set in and he fought it for a few days, thinking he was just suffering from the worst hangover of his life.

Then one day he had a craving. No amount of Alka Seltzer or full fat milk could quell the burning in his stomach. Without thinking, he went to the fridge, took out a large beef steak, ripped open the packet and started to feast on the raw meat. The old Skinner, somewhere in his head who liked his steaks well done, was repulsed at the thought of what he was doing. The new Skinner finished it off within seconds but the pain did not subside. He wanted more.

From that day forward, he had a compulsion to eat only raw meat, but while this felt natural to him, it failed to keep the hunger at bay. Visits to the doctor were fruitless: they couldn't diagnose his problem. It had been the height of summer but he seemed to suffer from sunburn a lot more than he usually did and he decided to change his shift as a security guard and work nights instead. He stayed inside all day, either sleeping or searching the internet for people with similar problems.

Eventually he made contact with a mysterious character on a chat room who said she could introduce him to hundreds of people just like him and make the pain go away. He had no choice.

Roxy was her name and she was very welcoming. She showed him a new life with people of his own kind. She showed him the superiority of his brothers and sisters and he bought into the whole way of life. She had given him his first taste of human blood. Part of him had been repulsed but it was the only thing that could satiate his hunger.

The new Skinner had ruled his head ever since but in the past few minutes, the old Skinner had started to talk to him again.

Help them, said the voice in his head, *you have to help them because they can help you. It's what you really want.*

79
Hunger

I fell to the ground and rolled over, trying not to scream or do anything to alert the soldiers outside the lab to my suffering. The pain in my stomach was excruciating. I had never been stabbed but I suspected that having knives thrust into my guts over and over would feel something like this.

Agent Simpson was the first to my aid. 'What's wrong?'

'It's my stomach. I don't know what's wrong, it just started this second,' I stammered.

'It's the hunger,' I heard Doctor Owen say, 'I feared this would happen.'

'Give me another shot,' I pleaded.

'It'll probably knock you out for a few hours again,' the doctor said, looking very concerned.

'I don't care how long I sleep for. The longer the better. Just do it,' I pleaded.

'No, wait!' shouted a voice that I didn't recognise.

I looked up and saw the soldier who had been left in the lab by Captain Stein walking over to me. He lifted me up and sat me down on an empty bed.

'What do you think you're doing?' asked Agent Simpson.

'Fight through it, Detective. The hunger will subside,' the soldier said to me.

'What do you know about it?' asked Agent Simpson.

'Listen to me, I know what I'm talking about,' said the stranger.

'You're a vampire, aren't you?' said Doctor Owen, more calmly than the situation dictated.

'Yes,' he said, 'but I want to help.'

In a flash, Agent Simpson drew her gun and pointed it at the soldier, who raised his hands and took a step back. 'Look, I just want to help,' he said, without a hint on insincerity in his voice.

'How long have you been here?' she asked.

'I've been a member of The Brotherhood for almost a year. I'm not the only one, you know.'

'We know there have been infiltrators. How many of you are there?'

'I'm not sure. I've sensed another two or three here but we're never told who they are. We have our missions and we carry them out, that's all.'

I've sensed another two or three, he said. I cast my mind back to the line-up of eight soldiers and my suspicions about the vampire infiltrator.

Do I have the same power to sense the presence of other vampires?

'What is your mission?' she demanded as I screamed again. It felt like my insides were burning away to nothing. The doctor walked over to me, carrying the syringe that I hoped would take me away from this agony.

'Don't give him the treatment, Doc,' the soldier said.

'Don't listen to him,' I shouted, 'I'm dying here. I know you want to help me but I can't take it any more.'

'This will hold back the effects of the virus,' the doctor said, 'why shouldn't I give it to him?'

'Don't listen to him,' said Agent Simpson, 'he wants him to turn into a vampire.'

'No, it's not that. You said it would knock him out for a few hours,' said the soldier.

'So what?' The doctor stopped to listen to the soldier for a moment. I really hoped everyone would get to the point so I could get the injection and go off to sleep.

'If you want to get out of here, I can help you, but we have to keep him awake and leave now.'

'How do we know we can trust you?' shouted Agent Simpson, still pointing the gun in the soldier's face.

'I guess you can't, not one hundred percent, but you have to have faith in me. I've already told you who I am. All you need to do is say the word and the Captain will come back in and force you to chop me up like you did to him. I take it you lot aren't here of your own free will? Don't you want to leave?'

Agent Simpson looked at the basins full of internal organs. 'Okay,' she said, 'the doctor will give Detective Ryder the treatment and we'll get out of here after he wakes up.'

'We can't wait that long,' the soldier said, raising his voice. He had an air of urgency that Doctor Owen and Agent Simpson weren't picking up on.

'Why not?'

'Because any minute now, the dead bodies recovered from Hartley House will turn into vampires and they're going to be just as hungry as your friend.'

80
Defection

'What the hell are you talking about?' Agent Simpson demanded, 'Any dead bodies recovered from battle sites are treated so they will burn if they turn into vampires.'

'The guy you chopped up is the one who treated them,' said the soldier, 'he was supposed to shoot the bodies with silver bullets but we switched the ammo with regular bullets.'

'So why do you want to help us if you're ready to set vampires loose in here?' asked Doctor Owen.

'I was carrying out my orders because I didn't know any better. As a vampire, I didn't think I had a choice. Now I've met you three and seen what you can do, I want to help. You're not like everyone else here.

'I had heard of Doctor Owen's work but the message I got was different. We were told that you wanted to kill all of us. I always hoped there was someone out there that could help us and now that I know there is, I want to be part of it. I don't want to be part of this pointless war any more.'

Agent Simpson thought to herself for a second and turned to Doctor Owen. 'That makes two of us.'

'I was hoping you were going to say that,' he said, 'I've had more than enough of these macho assholes.'

'Okay,' I piped up, struggling to get my words out, 'now we're all friends, what do we do? I'm lying here with my guts turning into mush, we've got masses of vampire bits to sort through and a squad of vampires in the morgue down the hall are starting to get hungry. How the hell are we going to get out of here?'

'We need to take care of those vampires first,' said the doctor, 'Private…?'

'Skinner, sir,' said the soldier.

'Private Skinner: go down to the morgue and finish off the vampires. I take it you can pilot one of the helicopters on the roof?'

'Yes, I've got one fuelled and ready to go.'

'Good. Agent Simpson and I will pack as much equipment and as many samples as we can fit into the steel cases we brought back from Hartley House. Detective Ryder: unless Private Skinner here tells us otherwise, you're just going to have to ride it out for now.'

That wasn't exactly what I wanted to hear. The thought of getting an injection and waking up far away from The Brotherhood a few hours later was very appealing to me.

'You said the pain would go away, didn't you?' I asked hopefully.

'It certainly won't get any worse. It'll subside in a while. As soon as we get out of here, the doctor can give you a shot.'

'I can hardly wait,' I said, remembering last night's dreams and questioning whether I would rather be unconscious or not.

Private Skinner checked his gun was loaded and made his way to the door, but was stopped by Captain Stein who bounded into the lab, followed by a pair of soldiers.

'Where the hell are you going, Private?' Before he could answer, Captain Stein spotted me perched on the edge of the bed clenching my stomach. 'Jesus Christ, he's turning, isn't he?'

'I can't say for sure,' said the doctor, 'I'm just going to have a look at him now.'

'Bullshit! Look at the state of him. He's turning into a bloodsucker and you know it!' Captain Stein's rage knew no bounds. Only he really knew what he was capable of.

'Then leave us alone to treat him!' the doctor shouted.

'Not a chance, Doc,' said Captain Stein, 'Strap him down.'

'What?' Agent Simpson exclaimed.

'Detective Ryder is your next subject, Doctor Owen,' said Captain Stein as he drew his gun and pointed it at the doctor, 'The son of a bitch is a vampire. Chop him up.'

81
Reborn

The door to the morgue had been locked and the soldier standing guard outside thought nothing of the two piles of body bags lying in the cold darkness in the room behind him.

One pile of bodies was decomposing.

The other twelve bodies were regenerating.

The pool of blood that had gathered in each body bag was slowly reducing in size. Vampire blood was finding its way back into the open wounds of the dead soldiers, which closed and new skin grew over the top, sealing wounds within seconds and removing all sign of scars. To look at them, no one would know they had been bitten.

No one would know they were now servants of the undead. Even the soldiers themselves didn't know why they had awoken. The last image in their minds was of a vampire bearing down on them and sinking its teeth into their neck.

One by one their eyes flicked open and quickly closed again as they gripped their stomachs with both hands and moaned in pain. Their insides were on fire. It felt like their internal organs were dissolving, sending intense heat to all corners of their bodies. The body bags shook as the newborn vampires writhed in agony.

They could sense each other's presence. Each soldier lying in a zipped-up body bag knew he had eleven blood brothers in the room. They all ripped open the body bags with little effort and felt a powerful warmth spread down their legs as they struggled to their feet.

Each one of them was being driven by one desire. The need to ensure their survival.

They had to feed.

82
Strapped Down

This is not happening. This is not happening.

First I get bitten by a vampire, then I get forced to join a fanatical group of killers and to top it all off, I'm going to be sliced open in the name of science.

One of Captain Stein's soldiers held me down while the other strapped me to the bed. Stein was wide-eyed and manic, brandishing his gun, threatening to shoot anyone who tried to help me.

Private Skinner was still armed though, our man on the inside from the other side. He was our only hope.

'What is your problem? Why are you doing this?' I asked Captain Stein, not expecting a reasonable answer.

'You've been bitten, Detective. You will turn into a vampire and I can't take the risk. Just over a year ago I lost an outpost in a vampire attack. It happened again last night. I swear I will not let it happen again. All you are good for now is parts for the doctor to run tests on.'

I had resigned myself to that fact several hours ago but I didn't want all my parts to be separated and experimented on at the same time. Dying wasn't part of the plan. Not at this point anyway.

'But the doctor can help him,' pleaded Agent Simpson, 'he's working on the treatment and we have already used it to slow down the effects.'

'How many times do I have to tell you, Agent Simpson? The primary treatment is the only way forward and it is the only treatment the doctor should be working on. I will not rest until every vampire is turned to dust. Now use this man's body to find a way for me to rid the world of this curse.'

Captain Stein was not going to change his opinion. He had already gone too far down the path of The Brotherhood and killing vampires was all he knew. His hatred was etched into his mind by ignorance and endless brainwashing by his superiors. It was too late for him to begin questioning his orders.

'There has to be another way. Killing this man will not bring us any closer to any kind of treatment.' The doctor tried in vain to bring a sense of reality back to the proceedings.

'Chopping this man up will provide you with more samples. The more samples you have, the better your chance of finding the primary treatment. You said that yourself. I don't want any excuses, Doc. Get to work.'

Just when I thought things couldn't get any worse, there was a series of loud bangs and a painful scream from outside the lab.

Is it the vampire soldiers? Have they been reborn before Private Skinner could dispose of the bodies?

'What was that?' exclaimed one of the soldiers.

'I'll go and check it out,' said Private Skinner, and headed out of the door after getting the nod from Captain Stein. He gave me a passing glance as he walked past me. This vampire was our only chance of getting out of here and he had run away to look for his brothers. I hoped he knew what he was doing.

Captain Stein ordered one of his men to strip me. The soldier leaned over me and ripped my shirt open. Doctor Owen reluctantly leaned over me with a look on his face that told me he didn't know how to get out of this situation. He looked into my eyes inquisitively and placed a finger on my lower jaw, opening my mouth. When he was sure no one else could see his face, he winked at me then reeled backwards.

'What's wrong, Doc? Stop stalling,' said Captain Stein.

'Look at his teeth,' the doctor said, his voice trembling.

Captain Stein leaned over again, but before he could look into my mouth, Doctor Owen grabbed him by his shirt collar and held a scalpel at his neck, pressing it against the flesh next to his Adam's apple. The soldiers gripped their rifles and pointed them in the doctor's direction but the looks on their faces told me they had no idea how to handle this situation.

'Get back!' the doctor shouted at the soldiers.

'You've no idea what you've just done,' said Captain Stein in a cool, assertive voice that contrasted the predicament in which he found himself, 'you can forget about your work now, Doc. You're a dead man.'

'That's wrong and you know it, 'said Doctor Owen, 'you need me to complete the work on the primary treatment. If that's what you want then that's what you'll get but I will not cut this guy up for no good reason. He doesn't deserve it.'

'Doctor Forrest's still out there,' said Captain Stein, 'you're not the only expert in this town. It's not like you've produced anything useful anyway.'

'How can you say that after all we've seen today? We have made giant leaps in understanding vampire anatomy. If that's the way you feel then I quit. I'm getting out of here.'

'You quit? You can't do that. I won't let you leave here. Agent Simpson, shoot the doctor,' Stein ordered.

'I'm afraid I can't do that,' she said, 'I agree with Doctor Owen. We should be focusing our efforts on the secondary treatment. I can't go along with your methods any more either. We're getting out of here right now.'

Doctor Owen turned to shout at the armed soldiers with a renewed sense of vigour in his voice. 'Put your weapons down or the Captain dies! Put them down now!'

83
Feeding

Private Skinner could sense the presence of vampires. They were very close. He heard a commotion from the lab as he turned the corner at the end of the corridor.

He considered turning round to go to his new friends' aid but realised that he was the only person who had a chance of taking care of the imminent threat.

The heavy metal door to the morgue was open. Not only was it open, it was hanging from its hinges and the soldier that had been standing at the door was no longer there. Private Skinner raised his rifle and moved forward in small steps.

There were no other rooms near the morgue, no other doors lining the corridor. The vampires had been reborn and the morgue was the only place they could be. There was nowhere else they could have gone without being seen by everyone in the lab.

Light was spilling into the morgue from the fluorescent lights in the corridor, illuminating the room and casting a long shadow of Private Skinner as he reached the doorway. He looked into the morgue, trying to adjust his eyesight to the darkness from the clinical white glare that lit the rest of the base.

For a few moments, he saw nothing but his senses told him something was lurking in the shadows. He closed his eyes and listened for a sign.

There it is.

He heard the sound he had dreaded but all the time knew was coming. The sound of tearing flesh, the slurping of blood.

*Someone, some*thing *is feeding in here.*

Private Skinner's eyes adjusted to the low light and he laid eyes on what he had heard.

Twelve vampires, all feeding on the body of the soldier that had been standing outside the morgue not five minutes ago, thinking that guarding dead bodies was the easiest job in The Brotherhood. The uncontrollable hunger of twelve newborn vampires meant that they had already reduced the body to almost a bare skeleton. Only a few pieces of dry flesh hung from the soldier's bones.

It was only a matter of time before the new vampires felt something click in their minds. They were becoming aware of a new talent: the ability to sense the presence of their new brothers and sisters. All at once, the twelve of them turned their blood soaked heads around to look at Private Skinner.

They all got to their feet and started to take steps towards the door. One more new talent hit them: the ability to sense danger. Even though they instinctively knew the man at the door was one of their brothers, he was not to be trusted.

Before Private Skinner could squeeze the trigger of his rifle, all twelve of them had scattered around the morgue, heading for the darkest corners they could find. The machine gun fire lit up the room for a second and the bullets rattled off the metal fixtures but failed to find a target.

Private Skinner knew he wouldn't be able to hold his own against these vampires with a rifle that was quickly running out of ammunition so he turned on his heels and made his way out of the morgue as quickly as he could. Unable to lock the door behind him, he kept peppering the doorway with bullets, hoping to keep the advancing vampires at bay but it wouldn't be long before they broke out of the morgue and overran the base.

As he turned the corner, he met a squad of four soldiers coming the other way. 'What the hell's going on?' one of them asked.

'Vampires in the morgue,' Private Skinner replied, 'Twelve of them. If they get out of there, we're all dead.'

'We can't let them get out then,' said the soldier as he flicked his rifle's safety catch. Private Skinner continued running in the opposite direction as gunfire behind him echoed down the corridor.

If he and his new friends in the lab were going to make their escape from The Brotherhood, it was now or never.

84
The Voice

I was lying on the bed, strapped down and looking up at the armed soldiers who were frantically looking at each other, desperate for someone to tell them what they should do. They were shouting at the doctor, telling him they wouldn't shoot him if he put the scalpel down. I heard Captain Stein shouting, saying we were all going to die anyway so the doctor may as well let him go.

Through the commotion, I heard the hushed voice of Doctor Owen. I couldn't see him but I could hear his voice echoing in my mind.

'You can break free of your bonds, Detective. You saw how the vampires channel their energy. Channel your energy to your arms and break free.'

I thought of the vampire the doctor had chopped up, then I concentrated on my arms. *Do I have the same power? Can I break through the straps with the same ease?*

I pictured my arms breaking free of the straps. As soon as I started to struggle, I felt a warmth flow through my arms. It wrapped around my bones and muscles and my arms felt like they were ready to burst with the pressure.

Without really struggling, the straps ripped like they were made from paper and my arms were free. I looked down at my feet and pictured them breaking free of the straps. The warmth moved from my arms, down through my body to my legs. The straps binding my legs also ripped apart.

'Holy shit!' exclaimed one of the soldiers, and turned his rifle towards me. No sooner had Stein shouted 'Shoot him!' than I leapt to my feet, snatched the rifle from the soldier's hands and smashed him in the face with the butt. With one blow, blood sprayed from his mouth onto the wall and his neck made a loud crack. He fell to the floor unconscious, his legs and arms twitching.

The other soldier took a step towards me and before he knew what had happened, he had received a blow to the nose from the butt of my rifle. Following up with a kick in the chest, he flew backwards, crashing through the lab door. That just left Captain Stein to deal with.

I turned to him. His face was a contorted mix of horror and anger. 'You won't get out of here, Detective. You won't even get down the hall. As soon as my men find you, they'll kill you.'

'That's why we're taking you with us,' said the doctor.

I heard the sound of gunfire from outside the lab. Private Skinner appeared at the door. The look on his face told me exactly what he was about to say.

'We have to leave. Right now.'

85
New Instincts

'You're with them?' Captain Stein shouted at Private Skinner, but the soldier and everyone else in the lab ignored him.

'Have they been reborn?' asked Agent Simpson.

'Yes,' said Private Skinner, 'they've just woken up and they've already fed on one of the men. A squad is holding them back down the hall but they'll be on top of us very soon.'

Skinner looked at me, seeing something in me that the doctor and Agent Simpson hadn't mentioned. 'My God, you look terrible. Are you okay?'

'I've felt better,' I said.

'You're really starting to turn. We have to get you out of here before you're completely consumed.'

'Wait,' said the doctor, 'we need to take the samples with us.'

I yanked Captain Stein's rifle out of his hands and pointed it at him. Doctor Owen removed the scalpel from his neck and started to work with Agent Simpson to put as many samples as possible into the steel boxes.

Private Skinner was standing at the opening to the lab where the door used to be. A squad of soldiers ran down the corridor to meet him.

'What's going on?' one of them asked him.

'Vampires in the morgue,' said Private Skinner, 'they sneaked in and now they've woken up.'

The soldier spotted me pointing the gun at Captain Stein and the tone of his voice changed. 'What's going on in here?'

'The Captain is one of them. He smuggled the vampires into the base with the dead bodies from the attack on Hartley House. We've arrested him.'

I was sure the soldier didn't buy it but more gunfire distracted his attention and he led the men down the corridor.

'Have you got everything?' Skinner asked.

'We've got enough,' said the doctor, 'let's get out of here.'

I took a step outside the lab and immediately saw the flashes of gunfire from the end of the corridor. Private Skinner led everyone away from the commotion. I saw the limp, bloody body of a soldier fly through the air, hit the wall and land in a heap on the floor, followed by another flash of gunfire.

A vampire soldier ran round the corner towards me. I looked closer and saw one of his arms was burning, leaving a trail of ash on the floor behind him. He was still running towards me as the burning took hold of his entire body. I raised my gun to shoot but his body had completely disappeared before I could pull the trigger and a cloud of ash hit me in the face.

A soldier appeared at the end of the corridor. 'Where did he go?'

'You got him. He's dead,' I shouted.

'Thanks.' He noticed the Captain being marched down the corridor by Doctor Owen. 'Hey, what's going on there? Where are you taking the Captain?'

'He's being arrested,' I said, trying to look convincing again, 'don't worry about it.'

'What do you mean, he's being arrested? For what?' He started to walk towards me.

'He's one of them. He's the reason we've got vampires in the base.'

'I don't believe you. What's going on?' He pointed his rifle at me.

'Look, we've got all this in hand. We'll take care of the Captain and you take care of the vampires.'

Trying to give an order to a soldier isn't a good idea at the best of times but it's definitely not recommended if his squad mates are being taken apart by a team of invading vampires.

'Don't you talk to me like that, you little rat. Who the hell are you to be giving me orders? I want to talk to the Captain.' He spoke into his radio. 'Colonel, get another squad down here, the Captain has been captured by the cop. Something funny's going on.'

'We're on our way,' was the reply from his radio.

Private Skinner tried to back me up. 'He's right. Captain Stein has been showing the signs of becoming a vampire.'

All this time, Captain Stein was keeping his mouth shut. Either he was resigned to helping us get out of the base, or, which I thought was the more likely option, he had something else up his sleeve. After all, this was only one soldier against four of us.

I pointed my rifle at the soldier. 'Get back to work, soldier.'

'Don't point that at me, you…' I didn't give him chance to finish his sentence before pulling the trigger and blasting his body with silver bullets.

'Oh my God, Tom. What are you doing?' said Agent Simpson.

I didn't say a word. I'd killed three soldiers without thinking twice about it. I'd have no problems killing more of them if they stood between us and freedom. Doctor Owen had told me the future of the human race depended on both of us staying alive, and I believed him.

We have to survive. Whatever it takes.

86
Watching The Massacre

Commander North stood in the operations room, his blood boiling as he witnessed the massacre of his men. With every scream he heard over the radio, he knew the vampires were making their way towards the summit of the base.

The two men in the operations team were trying to guide the soldiers around the corridors but the vampires were too fast for them. They would have sent more soldiers down into the base if there were any more to send. Within a matter of minutes they would all surely be dead.

Then North saw a small group running in the wrong direction. 'Why are they coming back up here?'

'They're not soldiers, sir,' said one frantic member of the operations team as he rubbed his eyes and stared at one of the many screens in front of him. 'That's Captain Stein, Private Skinner, Doctor Owen and the civilian male and female that arrived earlier, sir.'

'Shit,' North remarked, 'why are they coming up here?'

'Stein is unarmed, sir. It appears that Private Skinner is leading them towards the summit at gunpoint.'

'How many men are left down there?'

'Not many sir. There's only two or three left and the vampires won't take long to reach us.'

'Has Private Skinner made contact?'

'Negative, sir. He has not answered our attempts to contact him.'

Commander North weighed up his options and knew he had to take drastic action, even at the expense of Doctor Owen. *The vampires must not be allowed to escape, but there's something else going on here with Captain Stein and Private Skinner.*

'Lock down the base.'

'Sir, are you sure? That means…'

'I know what it means, soldier. Lock down the base then pick up your guns and follow me.'

87
Reaching The Summit

We ran as fast as our legs would carry us up the long sloping corridors of the base, working our way towards the summit. We managed to avoid all the soldiers running to help the squad trying to fend off the vampire invaders by ducking in and out of various rooms along the way.

As much as I didn't want to believe him in the lab, Private Skinner was right. The pain in my stomach was starting to subside. The buzzing in my brain that told me vampires were nearby had relented but I didn't know if that was because the virus was wearing off or if it was because we were just getting further away from the machine gun fire and screams behind us. The pessimistic realist in me suspected the latter.

'You're not going to get out of here,' said Captain Stein, finally breaking his silence as we slipped into an empty dormitory to keep out of sight of another squad of soldiers going to meet their maker.

'It's only a matter of time until Commander North hits the button to lock down the base. Every security door will close and you'll be trapped down here along with the rest of us.'

Captain Stein had been keeping far too quiet to not be hiding something from us. He knew the procedure all along and was biding his time waiting for the lock-down, but I suspected that we were close to the top of the base. We had been sneaking around for a while and I thought Captain Stein was trying to put us off as a last resort.

'But won't that trap your men in the same rooms as the vampires?' asked Agent Simpson.

'That's right. When they turn, they'll feed on the soldiers but all we have to do is leave the doors locked and wait for them to starve. Then we can pick them off one by one.' There wasn't a hint of regret in Captain Stein's voice.

'That's barbaric.'

'That's life, Agent Simpson. Can you think of a better option? Another more humane way of getting rid of them? God knows these guys won't be able to kill all of them.'

Agent Simpson didn't say anything. She just stared at Captain Stein like her eyes were burning a hole in his head. 'I thought not,' he snarled.

'Come on,' said Doctor Owen, 'we'd better keep moving. We're nearly there.'

Private Skinner picked up the pace and we kept up with him until we turned our last corner. We found ourselves in the main hangar, where we had entered the base only a matter of hours before. Ahead of us a cloud-filled red dusk sky peeked through the open door at the top of the ramp leading out to the summit.

Freedom.

With a metallic clunk, the door to the summit started to close and a loud repetitive siren started to wail.

'There it is,' said Captain Stein, 'we're now on lock-down. You may as well turn yourselves in now.'

I heard a gravely voice behind us bellowing over the siren. 'Captain Stein, what the fuck is going on?'

We spun round to face Commander North, who was standing with two soldiers. All three of them were armed to the teeth and had itchy trigger fingers.

88
Wiped Out

Things weren't going much better for the squad trying to deal with the vampires deep in the heart of the base. They had managed to kill seven of the bloodsuckers, but now the remaining five had split up and each had headed in different directions down the maze of corridors. Instead of a full head-on assault, they now had to search the labs and pick them off one by one.

The soldiers' numbers were also dwindling. There were bodies strewn all over the floor, some of them lying dead, their necks broken, others screaming in agony as they failed to pull themselves onto their feet with broken legs, arms and deep gushing wounds. The floor was awash with blood, which squelched under the feet of Colonel Evans as he edged his way along the corridors.

The attack had been swift and brutal. As soon as the first squad of soldiers had entered the morgue, they were wiped out almost immediately. The vampires had pounced on them from all angles, beating them with their newly discovered strength and flew out of the morgue to find their next victims.

The next squad to arrive managed to kill a few of them but didn't last much longer. Once they had turned the corner of the corridor, they scattered in many directions.

Colonel Evans knew that splitting up would leave them vulnerable to attack. If the vampires made a move from their separate positions towards the summit of the base, a soldier could kill some of them but one or two might be able to get past them. If that happened, then they would be chasing them towards the senior officers at the surface rather than holding them below ground.

If that happened, it would spell the end of the base. Everyone would die and there would be five new vampires on the loose. It would soon be getting dark outside and the vampires would be able to make their escape back to the city.

Evans opened the door to another lab, pointing his rifle in every direction until he was satisfied there were no surprises waiting for him. He stepped back into the corridor and saw one of his men at the end.

'This room's clear,' Evans announced.

'All clear up here as well,' the soldier said and waved to him. As soon as the words had left his lips, a vampire launched itself through the window of a lab further up the corridor. Before the soldier could fire a shot, his head had been turned a full one hundred and eighty degrees by the vampire's powerful hands, which then picked up the soldier's rifle and disappeared around the corner.

Colonel Evans gave chase. As he turned the corner, he wasn't expecting to see the vampire immediately in front of him, pointing the rifle at his chest. Eight silver bullets penetrated Colonel Evans' body before he hit the ground.

* * * *

The vampire felt the presence of approaching soldiers before it heard their footsteps. One was approaching from directly behind him but he could feel the presence of one of his kin in the same corridor. The sound of footsteps and a weapon being loaded was closely followed by a smashing window and a voice letting out its last scream.

That's one less soldier to deal with.

Another soldier was running down the corridor, directly ahead. Before he could shoot, another vampire had jumped out from a corner and with one hand, cracked his head open against the wall. His body slipped down the wall, leaving a bloody trail behind.

More soldiers were killed to his left and right. One had his neck broken and the other blew his own brains out while pinned in a corner.

Humans are so weak, the vampire thought to itself. *How could I spend so long as a human when I could have had powers like this?*

With all of the soldiers in the area dead, the five remaining vampires gathered together and started to run in the direction of the summit. They could all sense the faint presence of more vampires. Their sixth sense was guiding them towards two of their brothers.

As they got closer and closer, a deafening siren sounded and heavy metal doors at regular intervals along the corridors slowly began to close. They darted around the closing doors until they saw the red glow of the outside world disappearing behind a closing door.

If they were quick enough, they could just make it.

89
Help Arrives

'Answer me, Captain,' screamed Commander North as the soldiers grabbed the guns from our hands, 'what's going on? Why are there vampires in my base?' His voice echoed around the massive stone hangar.

'The vampires are casualties from the attack on Hartley House,' said Captain Stein, 'They were brought to the base by a vampire who had infiltrated the ranks.'

Commander North moved towards us but didn't lower the volume of his voice. 'And where are you going in such a hurry? Why aren't you armed?'

'The doctor, the detective and Private Skinner want to leave the base,' Captain Stein answered.

'The guinea pig? Not a chance.' Commander North walked up to me and looked my directly in the eye. 'Do you know how much pain we've been through to get to this point? Do you know how long we've waited for the doctor to complete his work?

'There's never been anyone like you, someone we can learn so much from so don't think you're ever going to get out of here. The contents of your body are more important than your life. The doctor is going to cut you up into as many tiny little pieces as it takes to find a way to kill these fuckers.'

The doctor stepped forward. 'I'll do no such thing.'

The commander moved over to stand toe-to-toe with the doctor. 'Yes you will, because if you don't, you'll end up just like your lab assistant.'

I immediately knew what he meant by that comment. We had been completely wrong about who had killed Danny Johnson and destroyed the lab at Mantek.

'It was you!' I exclaimed. 'You blew up the lab! Why?'

'The secondary treatment, Detective. It was a pointless diversion that was wasting our time and money. We had to take extreme measures to get the doctor's work back on track.' Commander North talked about killing the innocent lab assistant like it was nothing. Just the means to an end.

I was starting to feel intense heat flowing all over my body. More than anger at the methods of The Brotherhood, I could feel something unnatural happening inside me. I was terrified that I would turn into a full-blown vampire in front of the Commander. Even though he wanted the doctor to experiment on me, I was convinced he wouldn't think twice about turning me into ash if I became unable to control my urges as a vampire.

'But why kill my assistant?' the doctor asked.

'An acceptable loss. Your work on the secondary treatment had to be destroyed to refocus your efforts. He happened to be there. It was unfortunate but necessary to cover our tracks.'

'You're crazy,' said Agent Simpson, 'this is not what The Brotherhood stands for. Doctor Owen's work has shown that we can find a vaccine that will allow us to co-exist. That must be the primary treatment. The Brotherhood was formed by the need for the two species to co-exist.'

'That is no longer the view of The Brotherhood and you know that, Agent Simpson. The directives come from the top.'

'But you're a Commander,' she pleaded, 'You have influence over the decision makers. Tell them what we are working on and once they see what we have learned and achieved so far, they will allow us to continue.'

'I can't do that, ' said Commander North, 'it is the widely held view that the primary treatment can be developed a lot quicker and it will be more effective. I don't even know why I'm arguing with you. You're staying here and that's the end of it.'

When it felt like all was lost, I felt a new sensation surge through my body. It was the warm feeling of belonging and it was getting stronger. I looked at the door that led down to the lab. Just as it was about to finish closing, five bodies flew through the gap.

My vampire brothers are here to help me.

90
Mission Accomplished

As the door closed and the siren stopped, two vampires immediately headed towards the armed soldiers, who both fired silver bullets but failed to make contact. The soldiers were lifted off their feet and carried high into the air before being dropped. They both hit the ground on their heads, breaking their necks with a loud crack, leaving their heads pointing at an unnatural angle.

Commander North was shouting obscenities and taking pot shots with his pistol. His shots hit one of them, then another, then a third. For all his apparent faults as a leader, he was a good shot. He was certainly a man to be feared, whether you were human or vampire.

The remaining two vampires flanked the commander and flew in a circle around him, making it difficult for him to aim. He fired shot after shot from his pistol but failed to hit them. Before long, he was out of ammunition.

As soon as he started to reload, the vampires swooped down and grabbed him, lifting him off his feet. Hanging in the air only ten feet above us, one vampire held the commander's legs, the other held his arms and they fed on his aging body.

He screamed in agony and dropped his pistol, which shattered into many pieces as it hit the stone floor. Commander North's blood poured from his body and collected in large pools on the ground. When there was no more energy left in his body, he stopped struggling and screaming but the vampires continued to feed.

'What are we going to do?' asked Agent Simpson, 'As soon as they're finished with him, they'll come for us.'

The pain in my stomach hadn't subsided completely and my new instincts were telling me to join my brothers above and feed on the commander's convulsing body but I knew deep down inside me that I had to protect our small band of resistance. The four of us were a mismatched group of humans and vampires but we all shared one motivation: to rid the world of the conflict between vampires and The Brotherhood.

I saw the commander's silver sword hanging from his belt and knew I had to get up there. I had to kill the last two vampires and get us out of here.

I felt the blood drain all the way down my body to my feet. The muscles in my legs felt hot and tight, like they had been pumped up after months of training. I jumped into the air and immediately felt the blood rush back up through my body to my fingertips. I felt like I was flying. My body kept rising and rising. I reached the commander and drew the silver sword from his belt. The vampires looked up with shock on their blood-drenched faces. They didn't expect to see anyone else up there with them.

In one fluid movement I spun round, slicing through their heads with the commander's silver sword. They let go of the commander's body but I caught him by his collar before he fell. The blood spread evenly throughout my body and I slowly descended to the floor through a flurry of ash falling from the burning vampires.

The commander was still alive when I touched down. He was struggling to breathe though, let alone talk. We looked into each other's eyes.

Something struck me. If we were to leave this place and try to survive on the outside, we would need some leverage over the vampires and The Brotherhood.

I gripped what little hair the Commander had on the top of his head and swung my sword through his neck, separating his head from his body.

His body landed in a heap on the floor and I held his head in front of me, looking into his dead eyes.

Mission accomplished.

'Tom, what have you done?'

'I have an idea.' I said as I walked over the doctor, still with Commander North's head in my hand. I threw it to him and he caught it with both hands, splattering blood all over his coat.

'Put it in the box, we're taking it with us.' The doctor looked scared and confused but he did as I said.

'Trust me,' I said. The look on everyone's faces told me it would be a while until they trusted me again.

'What are you going to do now?' shouted Captain Stein, 'You've killed a commander of The Brotherhood. There are almost certainly more troops on their way here now and it's only a matter of time until they track you down. They will kill you all. You're too dangerous now.'

'I know,' I said and walked over to Captain Stein, still holding Commander North' silver sword. I swung the sword and cut off Captain Stein's legs just below the knees. He sunk to the floor screaming in agony.

'What are you doing, Tom? Stop it' shouted Agent Simpson. Private Skinner ran over and grabbed me by the shoulders but I turned round and pushed him away.

I returned to Captain Stein and held him down. 'Don't worry,' I said, 'your legs will grow back.' On that note, I opened my mouth to reveal my extended canine teeth and sunk them into his neck. Captain Stein screamed again. His painful cries satisfied my lust to inflict pain on him.

The blood pouring down my throat was warm and sweet. I had never tasted anything like it. I felt as if I could feed forever but it was short-lived. I felt many hands on my shoulders and I was pulled away from him. I wiped the blood from my mouth and I lay on my back on the cold floor of the hangar.

With the hunger of the vampire in me satisfied, the human in me started to talk to me again. I had killed four people in cold blood and cursed another with a terrible infection.

Dear God, what have I done?

91
Escape

Private Skinner hit the button to reverse the lock-down and we made our way out of the base. We ran across the summit of the mountain to a helicopter. I could feel my skin start to boil in the blazing sunshine as we jumped on board.

'Jesus Christ,' Agent Simpson exclaimed, 'look at your skin!'

The doctor looked at my face, which felt like I had been lying in the sun all day. In reality I had been in direct sunlight for about thirty seconds.

'Lie down, Detective,' said Doctor Owen, 'I need to give you another shot.'

Private Skinner sat down in the cockpit and started the helicopter's engine. His face did not appear to have been affected by the sun as much as mine. We lifted off and the doctor plunged the needle into my arm. I wondered if the treatment would make any difference.

Have I gone too far down the path to turn back?

In a few seconds I felt the treatment start to take hold and the familiar burning started to spread all over my body. Trying to ignore the pain, I reflected on my actions.

I had new powers. I could fly through the air. I had super-strength. I had psychic abilities.

In the hangar, the human side of me had been unable to control my actions. I had become an unstoppable killer with a lust for blood. I didn't want these powers though, not if it meant I had to feed on human blood to stay alive.

I realised the human community wasn't much better. The Brotherhood had become corrupt and had an agenda of hate. The only chance I had was to stick with these three people. They were good people who wanted the best for me and the rest of the human and vampire races. I felt my new powers drain from my body and tried to be hopeful for the future as I drifted into unconsciousness.

But somewhere deep inside me, a new instinct remained. It wanted me to keep these powers. It wanted me to join my new brothers and sisters. It wanted me to complete my rebirth as a vampire and stay that way.

Forever.

Epilogue

92
The Survivor

Night had fallen by the time reinforcements arrived at the base. Three gunships glided in through the mountains and touched down at the entrance. The heavy figure of General Graham stepped out of the leading gunship. Six soldiers jumped out of each gunship, drew their weapons and ran down the ramp into the base.

General Graham marched down the ramp behind them. He had been playing the call he had received over and over again in his mind. Their most remote regional headquarters had been overrun with vampires. Twelve bloodsuckers had somehow got into the base and killed everyone in sight. The only survivor was Captain Stein, who had made the call to national headquarters.

At least, he was a survivor when he made the call. *'Vampires have infiltrated the base. They killed everyone. Everybody's dead. The doctor and the test subject are gone. I'm dying. Come quickly.'*

That was three hours ago.

The soldiers scattered all over the base. Each soldier reported back on their radio whenever they found a body. The updates came through thick and fast.

A body was lying face down surrounded by a large pool of blood with a sprinkling of ash on top. General Graham had to do a double take as he approached it. The body would have been lying face down if it had a face, but this body's head was missing. Turning the body over, General Graham saw the stripes on the uniform and instantly knew whose head was missing. Next to the body laid a pair of legs that had been cut off at the knee.

My God, this was a massacre, he thought. There hadn't been an attack like this for a very long time. *The vampires must be working towards something. Something bigger than this. But what?*

General Graham picked up his radio and spoke into it. 'Has anyone found the doctor or the test subject?' All he got were negative responses, which meant they had either been captured or…

'Two of the gunships are missing, sir,' a soldier announced as he approached the general, 'the inventory states they have three but only one is present outside.'

'The doctor and the test subject must have escaped,' said General Graham, 'It is possible they are in some way responsible for this. The gunship has a tracking device on board. Find it.'

'Yes sir!' The soldier turned on his heels to march towards the communications office but noticed something on the floor. There was a lot of blood everywhere but the blood he saw in front of him was leading a trail into the office.

'What is it, soldier?' asked General Graham.

'This trail of blood. I can't believe I didn't see it when we got here,' said the soldier.

'A survivor?'

'Maybe.'

'Lead the way,' said General Graham, who followed the soldier into the office. The trail of blood went round the desks and stopped at a blood-soaked telephone lying on the ground.

'This must be where the call was made from,' said the soldier.

'That's right,' said General Graham, 'but if Captain Stein had been lying here since he made the call, you would expect there to be a big pool of blood. The floor's dry apart from a few spots.'

They both scanned their eyes over the floor and around the room. Where was the body that had left this trail of blood? Then General Graham felt something lightly tap him on the shoulder. He turned around but no one was there. He wiped his shoulder with his hand and looked at it.

Blood. Where…

Very slowly, General Graham raised his eyes and looked to the ceiling. He took a step back and exclaimed 'Oh my God!' The soldier turned round and looked up.

There was Captain Stein, seemingly stuck to the ceiling, looking down at them with vacant eyes and a ghostly white face. He didn't have any legs below the knees. Captain Stein opened his mouth to show his long pointed canine teeth and opened his arms out wide then dropped from the ceiling onto the soldier's back, clawing at his neck with his long, sharp finger nails.

Before he could sink his teeth into the soldier's neck, General Graham delivered a hard boot to the body of Captain Stein, who let go of the soldier and landed in the corner of the room. General Graham and the soldier both raised their guns and the vampire stopped moving.

'Don't move, Captain!' the general shouted, 'Are you okay, soldier?'

'I'm fine. Should we shoot him?'

General Graham first instinct was to give the order, but he looked into the eyes of the vampire. Was there any sense in turning Captain Stein into just another pile of ash?

'No,' he said, 'he was useless as a Captain but he may yet be of some use to us as a vampire.'

93
Emily

Emily Owen was lying in her private cell in the police station. She had been there for two nights in a row. Captain Nash came round from time to time to bring her food and water and to apologise for the broken air conditioning system.

It's like a sauna in here, she thought to herself as she looked out of the window and wondered how it could still be so hot after the sun had set long ago. She got up and moved around, trying to generate movement in the air but it only made her feel worse. The only other option was putting her in the public cell with all of the recent arrests. She questioned whether that might be preferable, if only for a few minutes to cool down.

She was relieved when the Captain had told her that he had heard her husband was safe and well. She had feared the worst when she heard about the commotion downtown. Somehow she knew he was involved.

Andrew had told her that if she ever fell into the hands of the police then someone would try to collect her. According to him, she would be safer on her own than with the police but if there was no other option; she would have to re-join him. She had been very scared when the police arrived to pick her up but after two days of sitting around she thought her husband was probably just being his usual over-protective self and that she would be fine once he came to collect her.

She had been resistant to Nash's questioning so far. He had only spent fleeting moments with her though. It seemed to her that he didn't have a lot of time on his hands and was always rushing off to deal with something else.

There was a knock at the cell door followed by the familiar voice of Captain Nash. He opened the small flap in the metal door and peeked inside. 'Emily, how are you doing in there?'

'Same as before, still baking. I must be nearly done now.'

'Again, I'm very sorry about this. As soon as we have a detective available to question you or we get rid of the suspects in the holding pen, we'll be able to move you. I don't think that's going to happen for a while yet though.'

'Can you bring me some more water please?'

'Of course. I'm just going to get your dinner so I'll bring plenty of water as well.'

Emily thanked Captain Nash and heard his footsteps move away from the cell door. Then she heard something else, something she wasn't expecting.

The sound of glass shattering.

Then a woman's scream.

Then a gunshot. Followed by another, and another.

The terrifying sound of gunshots, shouting and screaming seeped into the cell. Emily banged on the door.

'Captain Nash! Captain Nash! What's going on?'

There was no answer other than more screams.

She sat down on the bed and curled into a ball in the corner.

Something terrible is happening out there. It is anything to do with Andrew? Is this anything to do with me*?*

As suddenly as the noise had started, it stopped. There was silence from the corridor outside. The sound of footsteps made their way down the corridor and stopped at the door. The metal flap opened for a second, then slammed shut.

'Captain Nash?' Emily asked, her voice cracking with fear.

Again, there was no answer.

A key was placed in the lock and there was a loud clunk as the door swung open and hit the wall.

Emily didn't recognise the man standing at the door with blood dripping down his face. He was dressed in black with a sword tied to his belt.

There was no one alive in the police station to hear Emily's screams as he launched himself across the room and dragged her out of the cell.

94
The Scientist

Roxy ended the call on her mobile phone without an answer for the fourth time. There had been no contact from any of her allies at The Brotherhood's regional headquarters. She feared the worst. All the vampires she had trained to infiltrate The Brotherhood must have been killed.

Either the doctor had been killed in the battle or he had escaped, which meant they were starting from scratch again. The vampire community couldn't know for sure how much the humans knew about the biology of vampires.

Of course, the vampires were doing their own scientific experiments. They had their own agenda, something similar to the humans' plan but it would be ready to test far sooner.

Roxy lifted herself out of her chair onto a pair of crutches and hobbled down the dark hall to the laboratory door. It would be another day or so before her legs would finish healing completely after such a severe injury. She opened the door and took a step inside, telling the scientist working in the lab not to let her disturb him. She sat down on a stool on the opposite side of the workbench to the scientist and watched him work.

The scientist had two racks of bullets, a pistol, a small paintbrush and a small glass bowl of blood in front of him. One by one, he picked up the bullets, dipped the paintbrush in the bowl and coated them with a thin layer of blood. He then placed each bullet in the second rack to let them dry. When he had finished coating all of the bullets with blood, he picked one up and loaded it into the pistol.

'Let's see if it works,' he said and got to his feet. Roxy followed him out of the door and across the corridor, into the room facing the lab. The room they found themselves in was bare and well lit. The only furniture in the room was a wooden chair, to which a gagged and naked man was tied. His face was soaked with sweat and he was white with fear.

The scientist pointed the pistol at the naked man and pulled the trigger. He flew backwards and struck the wall behind him, falling into a heap on the floor, still tied to the chair. Neither the scientist nor Roxy helped him up. The scientist took a stopwatch out of his pocket and pressed the button to start the timer.

'How long until he turns, Doctor Forrest?' asked Roxy.

'Hopefully under an hour but I'm working on making it more fast-acting,' he said.

'When will we be able to execute the next phase of the plan?'

'The day after tomorrow.'

Tom Ryder will return

As the first copy of this novel is published, I will be starting work on the follow-up. Until it is ready to print, you can find me at the blog where this novel was originally published online or lurking around the forums at dvdactive.com

If you liked *Rebirth*, pass it on to someone else and spread the good word. If you didn't like it, keep it to yourself!

Thank you for reading *Rebirth*.

Scott McKenzie
s.a.mckenzie@gmail.com
http://rebirthnovel.blogspot.com

www.ingramcontent.com/pod-product-compliance
Ingram Content Group UK Ltd.
Pitfield, Milton Keynes, MK11 3LW, UK
UKHW041948190726
13854UKWH00004B/1849

9 781847 534125